REBIRTH

LILY 2022

KEPRESSNG ANTHOLOGY PRIZE

First Publsihed by
Kemka Ezinwo Press Ltd
No. 79 Udo Otung Ubo Street
Uyo, Akwa Ibom State.
Nigeria.

978 978 790 462 6(Paperback)
978 978 790 466 4(Ebook)

A catalogue record for this book is available from the British Library.

Cover design and Illustrations by Chimele Ezinwo of Chigirl Arts

To

All who celebrate African literature.

To all the authors who made this possible.

Welcome to the LILY version of the KepressNG Anthology Prize 2022.
The theme, REBIRTH, was to accentuate the need to survive. We're coming out of the COVID era that has marred our adventures, livelihood, relationships, etc., for more than two years. We look forward to renewed friendships, hopes and ideas.
We got ten (10) winners and more this time.
Interestingly, the stories were mostly about healing and in some sense coming of age.

Our judges were:

Efe Ogunnaiya is otherwise known as **@bookreviewbymo** on Instagram. She started her literary career reviewing e-books. So far, the books she's edited have gone on to be bestsellers.

Titi Oyemade enjoys reading and listening to music. She is currently a book reviewer for the Businessday Weekender newspaper, and her reviews have also appeared on The Newcastle Review website in the United Kingdom. While browsing the bookstore for books by Nigerian authors, a memoir, biography, or autobiography will almost certainly entice her into a reading binge. She owes her reading addiction to the book clubs, The Book Club Lagos and the Sunshine Book Club Lagos.

Agnes Kay-E is a Nigerian in the United Kingdom and the author of eight books, including Blossom in Winter, a bestseller. She writes contemporary women's fiction, fantasy, and new age fiction. Her latest is Anatomy of Harmony. She is presently working on another Contemporary Fiction. In her spare time, she sings and writes music.

TABLE OF CONTENTS

LOST AND FOUND

WYNONA SEABROOKE

I used to pray to God.

Every week, my mother would squeeze me into my best shoes - even though they pinched my toes - tie a ribbon in my hair and walk hand-in-hand with me to Sunday school. Worship was all in good fun:

- Dancing.
- Singing joyous songs.
- Colouring in pictures.
- Making little crafts, I'd proudly show my family.

It was easy - I loved God, and he loved me.

I used to pray to a god.

I wanted to be good. I wanted to be pious - but adolescence turned what was once black and white into a shifting kaleidoscope of grey. Waiting for marriage had seemed easy until he sat beside me, hand on my leg, whispering into my ear. Gone were the games of worship - now that I was no longer a child, I was to sit still and silent within the pews, to obey each and every rule, the weight of sin upon my shoulders.

I told myself I still loved God, but it wasn't true. In my heart, I feared him more and feared the consequences that that lost love could bring down.

I stopped praying altogether.

Religion was illogical, a fool's daydream to soften a cruel world, a pretensive shelter for the weak. I studied alone. I worked alone; if no divine intervention was coming, I could rely only on myself. I scorned those self-help books - a lot of mumbo-jumbos they were, capitalizing off readers' insecurities. But cynicism isn't content with consuming only what it's fed, and after years of bubbling beneath my surface, it began to eat me too.

I was falling away into darkness, with nothing left to cling to.

I began to search.

Religion still held no appeal, but perhaps I had been hasty in dismissing the self-help books. I began with the strictly factual, trying to understand the neuroscience of the brain that had let me down. Thoughts have power, I learnt - and I had sabotaged myself. I tip-toed deeper into the spirituality section, and for all its sugar-coating, the genuine truth rang out.

God or no god, my life would forever spiral downward if I didn't love myself.

I began to pray again - but this time, it was to me.

The grace and love we sang about in Sunday school, I learnt to show myself. I recognized that teenage shame I carried with me still and learnt to let it go. With the hard work that had advanced my career, I learned to apply to my inner life as well. As time went on, a simple realization dawned on me, that spirituality and religion are not the same. I may never believe in a god again, but souls require nourishment. Mindfulness, love, and peace – no one can truly thrive without them.

The path ahead is as long as life, and though that may have scared me once, it doesn't anymore. I may not be a monk or dreadlocked yogi, but, in my own way, I'm finding peace, at last.

Wynona Seabrooke. is a Biochemistry undergraduate and hopes to remind women of the strength they have within them through writing. She loves reading and spends most of her free time as a photographer and makeup artist.

YOUR TONGUE AND THE FIRE

TESTIMONY ODEY

You've died once before.

No. Twice. And every time you left the face of this earth, your mother rent apart her long white gown, cursed the evil spirits tormenting her and cried. Every time you left, your father accused your mother of not making enough sacrifices when you were in her womb and ignored her for some days until he came to his senses and realized it wasn't her fault. Every time you left, family members, relatives and passers-by accused your mother of being a witch who sacrificed her children in the mighty coven of some sick spirit. When you came back to the world the third time, your mother made sure you stayed, regardless of whether you liked it or not.

You remember the high priest making incisions on your body, cutting a little of your flesh open and offering your blood as a peace offering for the spirits that troubled you to let you go for you were just a child.

You were given a necklace to wear at all times because it supposedly held life preservation powers.

You were to wear it at all times, never removing it

from your neck.

You are getting used to the resentful looks some of your mates give you on your walk to the stream.

You are not shocked because you know the rumour spreading about – you are an evil child possessed by an evil spirit that cuts short your life, only to bring you back a year after. Your mates are scared that this evil spirit will contaminate them. You are quite sure that they even have orders from their parents to keep away from you.

Only three of your mates in the entire community socialize with you. You met Tobi on your way to the stream, Temi, on your way back from the stream and Tolu while hiding to watch other girls practice their dance steps for a local competition. You don't dance because the high priest says it is forbidden for you to. He says you will wake up the evil spirits who cease your life by dancing. You would love to dance, shake your legs and waist and smile as people watched you in admiration, but you fear it will never happen.

Ola thinks you're the prettiest girl in the village; you've heard the rumours, and they have shocked you to the core – the most handsome guy in the community thinks you are worthy of admiration. You wish you could talk to him, and you both could become friends, but you know it will not happen because not only do you think Ola is out of your league but also because his words have earned you the hatred of Bimbo, the chief's daughter. She has looked at you intently quite a few times on your way to the stream, and you have seen pure hatred and evil in her eyes. She has never talked to you, but you know that she observes you all the time and that deep inside, she is plotting something terrible, something that will sweep you off your feet, something you will never recover from.

Mother recites incantations and sings poems for you in the dead of night. She holds on to your hands and begs you to stay. She promises to be the best mother on earth. All you have to do is stay.

"I am too old and tired for rebirth. Years have I waited to have you, only to have you leave again and again. The first time, you had come as a fat chubby boy with a small mouth. But there was something special about you. You had a small red mark on the back of your neck. A few months later, you died, leaving me in complete misery. Oh, how I cried and prayed that like the maize and flowers spring forth in springtime, you would spring back into my life again.

A year later, I conceived.

You came as a boy again, a tiny one with quite large lips. What alarmed me most was you had the same small red mark. Then, I knew that I was being punished for perhaps the sins I committed when I was still a child, those little sins of lying and stealing. I wondered why a spirit would possess my child, take my child away from me!

When I got pregnant again, you came as a girl, a very beautiful one, but you still had that small red mark at the back of your neck. I ran to the high priest, and he touched my stomach with a red cloth and said you would live. I believed! And you did! He said something after the incisions. He said you were chosen by the gods to serve the oracle, so you'll move into his shrine at age sixteen. It hurts me to let you go, but he said the gods would bring me joy again through more and more babies. So, I am expectant, waiting for the rebirth of hope after you might have gone to serve the oracle."

You're turning sixteen in three days. You have grown to love your mother. You wished you didn't have to leave her and be a slave to the oracle. At the same time, you were profoundly grateful. Without the high priest protecting your birth, you probably would have been long dead and forgotten, and your mother would give birth to you again, but in the form of another human. You move your hands on your head, outlining the neat and straight rows. Tolu made your hair into all back. You have told three of them about your plight.

"Please don't go! I'll miss you...please," Tobi whispers, and you're tempted to defy your parents, to tell them you go nowhere on your sixteenth birthday.

"That old priest is just looking for a concubine. It's been years since our kinsmen have gone to war and captured any pretty woman that caught his interest. I love the peace our new king has brought us, for I hate the sight of death and war. Still, I wish our community was having one right now, so we could all run to another village, or another pretty maiden from another community would take your place," Temi says ruefully. You feel despair. You think of joining his pack of concubines in his house. It would be a major disaster.

"You can face whatever comes ahead. What doesn't kill you makes you stronger. I feel for you, my dear friend, but we all can do nothing as no one fights against the oracle or the high priest. We will barely see your face once you get there because every concubine of the priest or slave of the oracle becomes a sacred property of the gods. I'll do lots of prayers for you," Tolu says.

It is not easy. You do not wish to go, almost wish you could run somewhere very far away. It is a day before your sixteenth birthday, and while helping your mother fetch water from the stream for the last time, Bimbo emerges from behind a big bush and walks up to you. Deep inside, something tells you she has been waiting for you to strike when the iron is hot. Her curvy waist swings madly, and you wish your waist was not so tiny… you still wonder how Ola can think you are the prettiest girl. Bimbo stops right in front of you, her hands on her waist, and a slow smile climbs her lips.

"Oh, hail the prettiest girl in our town," she mockingly says and chuckles.

Your clay pot stays steadily on your head, and you wish you could hiss and walk past her. She has done enough ignoring you for almost all your life in the village.

"I wonder when you will die…oh wait, you never truly die. You just keep coming back in new human forms. This is like your third life now, right? As well as the longest you've stayed. I have news from credible sources that you can be killed ever so easily if a single piece of item was taken away from you."

You bite your lips, saying nothing, not knowing where she's driving at, trying to guess her next move but failing. You feel like running, but you will not because if you do, she will think you are a coward.

"You evil, ugly thing…you think you can take away Ola from me?" she questions, and you notice she balls her fists.

"I've never tried to take him away from you or anyone else." You find her accusation ridiculous. "He's never talked to me for even a day."

She laughs without humour. "And now, he never will talk to you." She plunges her hands forward, and the necklace is torn from your neck. You know you will come back again because you can never truly die, but for now, you feel yourself slipping away, far away into a world big and dark.

Testimony Odey is a Nigerian teen writer, poet, and artist. When she is not reading or writing, you can find her watching Nollywood movies or scrolling through social media, where she encourages fellow Christians and makes new friends. Her first book, Uloma, won 2nd place in the Nigeria Prize for Teen Authors 2021 (Prose Category) and is currently being published.

MIRAGE

SEUN AKINTARO

Ngo

Ngo is just thirty-two this year. She is still in her prime but has never conceived since she got wedded to the one she was betrothed to six years ago. What could have caused her unfruitfulness? Is that the cross she had to bear or her destiny? But that has never occurred in her lineage. Who on earth has she offended that had refused to bury the hatchet? These and many other questions she had found no one to answer have always run through her mind.

She had tried all means to have her own child, but fate had denied her. As an Igbo woman, though civilized, religious, and elite, she had drank countless concoctions prepared by her village herbalist, which she got through me, her driver. Her husband had warned her several times never to believe in any fetish means. "It is only Almighty God that can bring about true rebirth" has always been the emphatic words of her husband. But what would a barren woman do? Her relatives, who should have stood by her while in this misfortune, had neglected her. Even her parents! Why would they? Are they not her parents?

Ever since her parents set their eyes on Akanji, her

husband, on the day she brought him to the village to meet her people, they have been nostalgic about their daughter's decision to marry a Yoruba man. They had never supported the union from the onset.

"Don't you see an Igbo man around? Or is it civilization that has blindfolded you?" was her mother's remark. "What do you now expect, now that her womb has refused to accommodate a foetus?

The last time she discussed the issue with her people, 'didn't we warn you' was their reply. That was the second year after her marriage. Therefore, she has decided not to go to her village any longer since her mother-in-law, Mama, who culturally is supposed to be cruel to her, has been truthful since likewise her husband. I know all these since I have been her driver for six years. She hides nothing from me.

The irony of life; Ngozi had never known any man till she met Akanji at the University of Ibadan, where they both had their first degree. They met at an academic seminar meant for University Scholars in their fourth year of study. Virtually all lecturers in the Faculty of Arts know Ngo for her good conduct and her brilliancy. Little wonder her name came out as one of the University Scholars to be awarded a scholarship, same as Akanji. From there, they got to know each other, and the inferno of their love was kindled.

Like I said, 'the irony of life, Ngozi, a slim, beautiful and fair Igbo lady, had always turned down countless proposals to marry her from numerous rich men from her clan and even some lecturers back in school days.

With respect and decorum, she dissented to any requests for her hand in marriage. No man had ever dared to harass her sexually, perhaps, not to lose their respect for her. It is therefore obvious that Akanji met her at home. How do we then explain this? Even prostitutes who had lost count of aborted pregnancies still give birth to twins. Mentally unstable women aimlessly walk on the streets and are in no need of a child conceived. Why was it hard for a woman who had been undefiled before marriage?

To hit the nail on its head, the sudden change of Mama just this morning propelled me to decide that it wasn't black and white. This Monday morning is really not a good morning for Ngo.

God is truly God!

Mama

Mama clocked sixty this year and had decided not to return to the village but to stay with Akanji, until Ngozi gives her a grandchild and makes her a 'true grandmother'. Before this, she'd visit Ibadan to spend a few days with the duo and give them words of encouragement before returning to the village. This time, she got in yesterday evening from the village with a few of her luggage not long after I brought *Oga* and Madam from the church evening service. With a receptive heart, she embraced Ngo and even prayed for the couple. Since they take me as one of them, we ate together at the dining table, cracked jokes, and talked at length until we slept off at the same spot. Nature can't be denied, I supposed.

I still can't find a clue to what had transpired within that very short hour to this Monday morning that had made Mama to wage war against Ngozi. Just this morning! Still like a stage drama. The former called the latter names: 'witch, prostitute, dog, barren woman' and thereof…

"Release my son from where you have tied him, and as you do that, remember to wipe away the fog you spelt on his face.

He is the only child I have; I need to see my grandchild before I go to the great world beyond to join his father. Rebirth is all I crave for!" Mama pleaded.

Ever since Mama lost her husband a few months to the birth of *Oga* Akanji, Mama had shared the role of a father as well as a mother. She had decided not to marry anymore but to stay strong, struggle and give her son the best. Little wonder she named Akanji after her late husband. She believed her husband had come to inform her of the new baby. Mama's dream has always been to play with her grandchildren and be called 'mama'.

When Akanji brought Ngozi home while in courtship, Mama gladly accepted her and never objected to their union, despite the fact that Akanji had vehemently refused to marry one of Mama's best friend's daughters, Mama still blessed their union. She would always want to see her Akanji happy. But why this sudden change this morning?

Akanji

Akanji Babatunde Adekunle, Mama's only child, a senior lecturer at the University of Ibadan, where he'd graduated. *Oga* Akanji was born not with a silver spoon. So, he had to struggle together with mama to make ends meet.

Mama had once said a few years back when *Oga* Akanji finished his PhD that her son had always been hardworking and focused right from his childhood days. There is even lettering on the wall of his bedroom which reads thus:

> ***"TO BE SUCCESSFUL, YOUR FOCUS HAS TO BE SO INTENSE THAT PEOPLE THINK YOU ARE WILD."***

He has taken his academics just like food right from the onset and wouldn't allow anything to distract him. Little wonder he won the annual National Cowbell Essay Competition at age seventeen while in High School. His school management then decided to sponsor his degree to make the school proud.

That same year he finished High School, he proceeded to study Civil Engineering at the University of Ibadan. Just like his wife, he was respected by lecturers and students for his academic prowess. The university later sponsored his master's degree programme, and he was retained as a lecturer afterwards. It was after he got this job that he and Ngo got wedded. From my view, he would have completely made Mama proud if his wife had given her a grandchild in the real sense, perhaps.

There was a time *Oga* Akanji and Ngo suggested that Mama should move from the village and join them here in Ibadan.

Mama diplomatically objected: "I am contented with where I am. Make I no come cause kata-kata for your house" has always been her reply. But why this sudden kata-kata this Monday morning?

I was about to walk into the living room to ask *Oga* about the car we would be taking to work when I heard Mama's voice. I opened the door and met the trio in this drama.

"If she has a child, she will know the value of early Morning breakfast for children" She turned to Ngozi. "Give me a grandchild if not grandchildren."

Ngozi closed her eyes.

"All you do is to eat apple. The apple that your children supposed to eat."

Like the Russian invasion, Mama sent her deadly word missiles, tongue-lashed her and called her all sorts of names I mentioned earlier. Yet, Ngozi never uttered a word but went back into her room with tears. I marvelled at the scenario. I wished the director of the 'stage drama' could cut that scene. I tried to say a word, but mama's temperament denied me a say. I, therefore, took the role of an audience immediately. I quietly went out and stayed near the window-side and peeped. Seeing Ngozi cry, I wonder how the storyline will eventually end. Besides, the title I should give it… a mirage?

From where I peeped, Mama's voice could still be heard.

Akanji sighed heavily. "But why mother? Why this sudden reaction? I have always known you to love Ngozi even more than you love me. This is not the first of your visit, mama. You seem strange this morning, and I don't really like the way you talked to that innocent girl."

Mama whispered. "Akanji, don't see me as a frustrated and wicked mother. I have reasons for all my actions."

"What reason would make you hate her so much?"

Mama adjusted her seat. "The kingship rule has fallen on you. And before you can be crowned as king, you must at least have a child. There must -"

"Have I told you I have interest in such? Mama."

Mama sarcastically cut in. "I am not saying that you should be interested; all I fear is the repercussion."

"How do you mean?"

"It is believed that the family who refuses the title will be cursed. More so, if the mother of the king-to-be is alive, she will be enslaved in the palace. Do you then want the mother who suffered for you to be enslaved?

Surprised, Akanji gasped, "Ah-ah! What kind of law is that? In this twenty-first century –"

"Look! Call it thirtieth century, tradition is tradition, and culture is culture. There is no place you can run to hide your head."

"How does this affect my wife?"

Ngozi is already at the door. She had concluded to go and apologize to mama and allow peace to rain when she heard mama's soft voice.

Mama shifted, and enthusiastically continued, "Thank you. It's believed that the prospective king must have at least a child so that he can know the sufferings of children and hears the cries of mothers. If not, a woman will be forced on him!"

"What? I am a born-again Christian, and my religion doesn't support that."

"You had better calm your nerves down. There is a solution. The solution is even in your *shokoto*. Look at you, a young promising senior lecturer like you must surely have a lot of female students on your campus wanting to be your flirts." Mama paused dramatically. Smiling, she added, "You can invite any of them, and you know."

Maami! Where then should I put Ngo? I should send her packing? Ehn?

Showing innocence Mama mumbled, "No o! Ngozi is still my daughter-in-law. Our fathers say, 'it is the destiny of a child that calls for the arrival of another.' Marry another wife that will give me a grandchild. Take out of your female students, Akanji. Wake up, boy."

From where I was standing, I was certain that Ngozi had heard their conversation, so I moved toward her window to see what was next. Ngozi locked her bedroom door behind her and began to soliloquize and pace.

"After all, I did for this woman and for her son, I must kill this woman."

That was all I could faintly hear. She thought for a long time. Finally, she stops, then she brings out of her wardrobe a pack of bread and injects the bread with a syringe. My instinct notified me that a bad occurrence was about to be unleashed.

Ngozi then came out of her room, now shedding crocodile tears to apologize to mama. She knelt and asked mama to help her find a solution to her plight, not minding its aftermath. After that, she went into her room and brought out the bread on the dining table. There, I know Ngozi's ambition to kill mama is not a mirage. She is now desperate. Ngozi had already known that her husband would have lost his appetite for food since mama had already destabilized him and that mama would want to eat the bread alone since bread is what she likes most when it comes to food. Will she now eat the poisoned bread?

Mama quietly moved to the dining table to take her breakfast after all the energy she had consumed on waging war on her daughter-in-law. I couldn't hold my peace any longer at the spot I was. 'I have to do something drastic quickly', I thought. As mama was about to take the first loaf of the bread, I barged in, shouting. The loaf of bread on mama's hand fell on the ground, but some were already in her mouth - not yet swallowed though.

"Don't swallow that bread, mama!" I cautioned.

"It's poisoned."

I was just shouting 'poison' until a slap landed on my face, which put an end to my temporary death. It was then I realised I was dreaming all day long. *Oga* Akanji's slap woke me from my slumber. He and Ngozi are already set for work; even mama had taken her bath just to come out of her room to take her breakfast. Without being told, I knew I'd slept off at the dining table after last night's dinner. It was from there that the story of mama's cruel behaviour at Ngo began.

"What arrant nonsense is this, Akpan?" *Oga* questioned me.

"So, if I hadn't woken you, you would still be eating poison in that your stupid dream -"

"I wasn't the one that ate poison sir. It was Ma... I tried to give him a full detail of my dream."

"You had better tidy up and drive us to the hospital!" *Oga* yelled at me.

"But sir, today is Monday. We should be on our way to your place of work and not to the hospital," I replied.

Then I heard mama's voice. Mama was restless. "The doctor just called your *Oga* that the pregnancy test Ngozi did last Thursday is out. She is three weeks pregnant."

It sounded like a fairy tale to me that I didn't know when I was shedding tears. Oga's wife, Ngozi, has been fruitless for six years.

Why now?

So, I drove them off to the hospital. While I was at the wheel, I narrated the whole dream to their hearing and getting to the poison part; Ngozi landed me another dirty slap as she asked:

"Why would I kill my mother-in-law? My heaven on earth."

God is truly God. It is only Almighty God that can bring about true rebirth indeed. Human diabolical ways are mere mirages. Ours is no longer a mirage. It's real. This is the good news we have been waiting for. So, I took my *Oga*'s wife's slap with a smile.

THE STRANGER

ELIZABETH NAFULA

Sakula woke up. She stretched her arms and got out of bed. She cleaned her teeth and put on the iron. The heap of clothes was about to make her run mad.

"Does she think I'm a house help? Why would a grown-up think of giving a little girl like me such a heap? At times, she lacks something between her ears. I am doing this now that my father had reached his threshold when it came to raising a daughter. After my mother died. "

Sakula listened to Aunt Gloria's voice calling, and that's when she remembered she'd left the iron on. The smell of a burning piece of cloth was slowly spreading. Sakula looked at the only wire that was left hanging on the extension.

"How am I going to explain to Aunt Gloria? She won't give me a chance to defend myself," she cried quietly, her shoulders heaving up and down. She wipes her face with one end of her dress.

"Sa...kuu...la...! What's burning?"

Sakula moved a step forward, then stopped. The tall, slender girl bit her lip continuously as if she had been waiting for Aunt Gloria to speak. She pressed her feet on the tiled floor and glanced around to see where her aunt might come from. Her toes, curled into each other. Her face had a look you see on people ready for war with no weapon; next to her right elbow was a fresh scar from a fire burn. She straightened her arms like legs on wooden stools to prevent Aunt Gloria from seeing the burn.

"Why are you taking long to get out of that room?" Aunt Gloria shouted at her and began yanking on the door. She pulled as hard as her flabby arms could manage, inching the lock out a bit each time. Her dress stretched and tore from the slit to the waist. She kicked her right foot, kicked the left and finally rested her whole body on the door. Quite suddenly, the entire thing flew off; hinges displaced, sending the nails in the opposite direction. The door dropped right in front of Sakula's feet, followed by Aunt Gloria's body of an athlete. The lock was the only thing she carried.

"Young man, are you a statue? I have been calling your name for over five minutes, but no response."

Sakula shifted her gaze to the room window, tears playing hide-and-seek in her eyes.

"She just called me man?" Sakula was setting out the best way she could respond to her. Aunt Gloria tilted her head to face her. Sakula prepared herself to receive the harsh words that were about to come out of her mouth. She noticed from the rattling of her incisors.

"A woman who has a hoarse voice, beards, and many other manly features, is a man!" She finished her statement by holding Sakula's right arm. She rotated it to breaking point and pushed her on the seat next to the door.

Sakula dropped on the chair, hitting her back on the newly painted wall. Her mind clocked to death. Even if she screamed or cried, her aunt wouldn't care. It was better for her to save her breath; maybe she would survive for a couple of days.

Sakula rested for a while, then reached for the window. She watched the cool air filter through the window into her eyes. She was tugging at the curtain and peeping through the window to see if there was a sign of a human who had come to rescue her.

"The words my aunt uttered this morning have broken me down. Is it my fault? Who is to blame? I grew up knowing I am female. Why did she accept to live with me in the first place?"

The sudden yanking of the door sent her toward the broom; she picked up the broom and pretended to sweep. She listened to the knock for the second time, "Who are you? Why are you persistent? Aren't you certain that's a door made of wood?"

"I'm Tobi."

"Tobi? What a name!"

Tobi yanked the door again, attempting to pull the lock, peeping through the keyhole.

"I'm off to the kitchen."

Sakula set the water on the gas cooker to boil. Tobi knocked once and sat on the grass. The breeze coming through his nostrils made it unnecessary for him to fan himself. He admired how the leaves and branches of the trees danced to the flutes of the wind. He looked at the door, checking if it was open and threw his legs out of the compound.

Sakula focused her ears on the footsteps and knew her aunt was coming. The *sufuria* pan she had set to boil was burnt, and that was when she remembered to turn off the gas cooker.

"Sakula!"

Sakula was shaking uncontrollably.

"Did I hear somebody knock?"

"I didn't hear," she lied.

"You, man, better go to the farm now." Aunt Gloria fired a slap at her. Her chest started to shrink to the size of her fist. Sakula looked at her aunt with a question on her face. Her aunt looked back at her with the answer on her face, and she picked the broom to sweep. Aunt Gloria circled back around and was carrying a whip. Sakula pushed up against her and splayed her legs and arms like she was defending a fight.

"You don't have to punish me." Sakula got hold of her skirt, pleading with her.

"Stupid. You don't know the woman you're dealing with. As much as you are manly, I'm athletic."

The heat of their collective exchange landed at her nostrils. The rising voices closed the gap between what she said and what Aunt Gloria said. The words wanted to break the boundary. The violence of their speech spread across her shoulders and inched down her backside. Sakula folded her arms up.

Tobi invited himself early in the evening. Sakula neither looked at him, not responding to his greeting.

Aunt Gloria pretended as if nothing had happened and rested her chest on Tobi's.

"Is this Aunt Gloria? The woman who talks ill of men? She is a pretender."

Sakula looked at them as if her next action was to take a _panga_ (machete) and slice them.

"Get in and prepare dinner for the visitor."

Sakula listened to Aunt Gloria and Tobi's conversation. She threw away the knife in her hand that almost pierced her foot when she heard Aunt Gloria call her.

She materialized from the kitchen where she had been eavesdropping on their conversation. Tobi took off his shirt silently. Sakula blocked her eyes with her arms. Aunt Gloria massaged his back. Thereafter, he leaned back so that he rested on her arms. His stomach exposed wasn't a good picture in her eyes. Sakula walked to the kitchen and entered the room carrying a large tray with bowls of white rice and chicken bones. She hit her foot on the table and nearly fell next to where they sat. Tobi took the tray and requested for a serving spoon, then cradled his plate, inhaling the aroma of the food.

"Come. Sit here. I want to introduce you to the visitor." Her aunt motioned to a blue plastic chair supported by the wall.

Aunt Gloria entered her room and left Tobi and Sakula in the living room.

The lull loomed the room for over thirty minutes.

"Don't sit far away from me," Tobi began.

"No, have some manners," Sakula curtly replied.

"Sorry. I have noticed something strange in you. Are you male or female?"

Sakula looked at Tobi and read from his face that he was prepared to listen to her and even willing to help.

"I'm female," Sakula replied with the confidence of a warrior who had just killed a lion.

"I have noticed you have a hoarse voice. And again, you got beards. Your physical appearance is more of a male person."

"I never realized that. How did you discover all that?"

"It's an observation. I can help you out only if you decide whether you want to be male or female."

"I was born female. I have been for twenty years."

"Very well."

Sakula stared at Tobi, "Can you please tell me how to seek treatment?"

"It's simple. I got the medicine."

"Can I swallow it now? I'm getting impatient."

"Yes, but again... I'm afraid if your aunt finds out. Then, you'll have to take a rest for six hours after swallowing them."

"I'm ready, please..."

"If you follow the instructions, your voice will suddenly become soprano, and the beards will diminish right away."

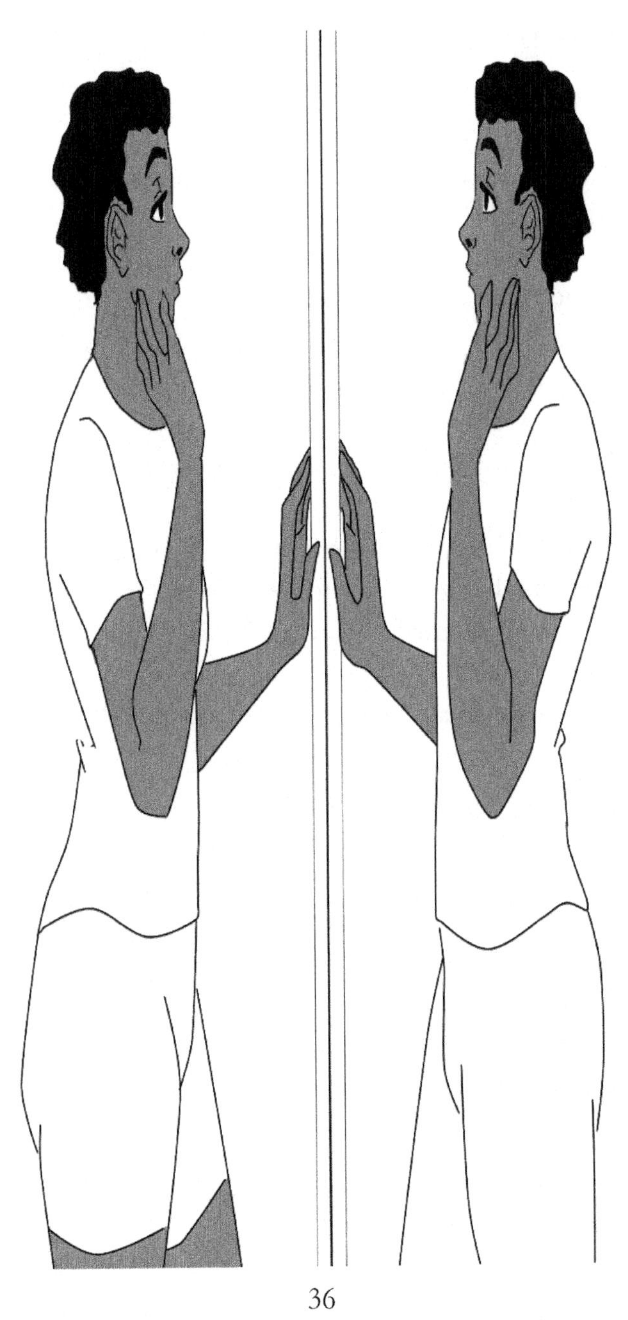

"I'm female. I can never be male."

The night was restless. The darkness seemed to exceed. Sakula had to twitch her eyes often to keep her from sleeping. With her head bowed, she didn't glance to her left or right. She kept thinking of what Tobi had told her. She scanned the whole sage of her being a hermaphrodite. No one entered the room. No one left the room. She was mixed up. She wanted to cry. But she did nothing instead.

Tobi unzipped his small bag and took out the medicine packed in a khaki envelope. Sakula felt like she was in another world. Anyone watching her facial expression would conclude she was certainly happy. She filled the glass with warm water and swallowed the medicine.

Sakula dropped to bed in the excitement of being a female the following morning. On waking up, she first made for the mirror. Her beards we're missing. Her voice was soft, and her body appearance changed.

Sakula cleared her throat and pushed out the loudest voice," I am finally female."

Aunt Gloria came running," Who is in this house? I thought it's you, I and Sakula in here."

Tobi hid his smile and marched out of the room to prevent Aunt Gloria from suspecting him. He sat on the bench next to the guava trees. They dropped one after another as though they were happy Sakula was now a female. Aunt Gloria made her way to Sakula's room and found her singing. She nearly dropped back after listening to her soft voice.

"This isn't Sakula! The man."

Tobi was figuring out how to call Sakula. She, too, was figuring out how to leave her room. Aunt Gloria didn't like the idea of Sakula transforming into a female. Tobi entered the house, picked up his bag and looked at Aunt Gloria, thinking she would see him off. Sakula listened to the movements and came out of her room.

Sakula held his arms and knelt next to him. "Sorry, Tobi. I ignored your knock when you visited earlier yesterday. I didn't know that you would help me this much."

Aunt Gloria looked at Tobi, then at Sakula, and sneered as she walked out.

Elizabeth Nafula is a writer, teacher and research enthusiast with a deep passion for books and literature. She divides her time between scripting and reading fiction stories. She has authored a Novella Silence is Gold and is currently working on short stories. Elizabeth is also a playwright (stage plays).

DAWN AND DUSK

NUSRAT OLOLADE LASISI

Today was the most sought day of my life.

It was my convocation ceremony. Five years of studying and unending pursuit now comes to an end. I had always had my eye on the prize- emerging the best student of the year. Melinda and Thomas, my best friends since matriculation, were seated beside me. As we progressed into the school auditorium, amidst the crowd, parents, and well-wishers, I felt a tear drop from my eye. This was the day my father looked forward to. I remembered the day he purchased the last JAMB form for me. I had been denied admission twice. But he kept cheering me on.

"Fareedah, don't worry, this time next year, you'd be given law in Lagos. Just keep pushing."

"Father, let me just study English language that was given. I am tired of staying at home," I replied.

"And become what? Bitter? Why don't you patiently wait for the course of your dream rather than study what is given."

"But Father..."

"No, my dear, I won't watch you become bitter in

the future. Start preparing for the next JAMB. I will call Santos to start tutoring you."

True to his words, I was given admission at the third attempt to study law. Father's joy knew no bounds. He had even, out of joy, organized a small gathering to celebrate my achievement.

"Fareedah Femi is the first and only female to be given law as a course of study in a federal university, in this family. And by the grace of Allah, she shall graduate as the best in her set."

"Amin!" echoed all in the dining room. Mother was equally excited, and she served all guests eagerly. But father didn't live to witness this day. He died when I was in my second year. Perhaps, it was for the best he hadn't witnessed today.

As the registrar called on the best graduating students in each faculty, I became nervous for no reason. Yes, I deserved this fear. I worked exceedingly hard, burnt the *mid*night candle, and did all I could. I did not only emerge best in my faculty and department. I was also the second-best graduating student in the institution.

"The best graduating student from the faculty of law, Miss Fareedah Femi."

There was thunderous applause as I stepped out of my seat. Mother arose quickly and hastily walked behind me. Her Nixon camera, which she bought for this event, was in her hand. Her purse was in between her armpit and bosom. I looked behind and could see my biggest fan cheering me on. My siblings, Maheer, Malik, as well as Fathia, were seated on their chairs but kept clapping and smiling. Mother must have instructed them not to move. If the school had allowed it, mother would be spraying newly mint notes while I walked. I mounted the podium and received my award. Mother beckoned on Maheer, my undergraduate sibling, to come take a photograph while we were presented the award. Mother held it tight like it was her life.

"Congratulations Ridah," Melinda said.

"Babe, you did it," Thomas added as he hugged me while I took my seat. I was happy. My phone vibrated, and I saw it was a message. I believed it was a message from a well-wisher, but it turned out to be Musa's, my toxic ex.

"Congratulations, babe. Even though you refused to grant me my wish, I still wish you well. However, I have a little gift for you and here's a countdown. Congratulations, babe."

What a psycho, I thought. But what gift did he have? This guy meant no good, and whatever he was up to would be bad. I brushed the message aside and concentrated on the registrar. Soon, it was time for the Chancellor to present awards and gifts to the top three graduating students. All of a sudden, there was a vibration from my phone. I looked at the screen and saw a timer on it. I knew it was Musa; he was a computer wizard and psychopath. What was he up to? I hesitated to call him but decided not to. Calling him would be fuelling his toxicity, so I turned the phone over.

The Chancellor then called the third best student

from the faculty of humanities, and social sciences, awarded her, and then took the photo. Her parents were there with her, and I was sad because of my father's demise. Next, it was my turn. As I was about to rise, the timer began to count down from sixty seconds. I became apprehensive. Then, the Chancellor called my name. Suddenly, fear came over me and I felt like hiding. But I looked at my mother's smiling face and felt assured again.

"That's my daughter," she said proudly. This time, aware of the prizes, she gave her purse to Fatiha and ordered them to approach the podium for a family picture. When I arrived at the podium, the timer was left with five seconds, and it was loud, so I quickly reached for it to silence it, but it wouldn't. I became nervous instantly, but it didn't matter.

As I stretched out my hand to receive the handshake from the Chancellor, the timer read zero, and then there was a crack on the projector. We felt it was a signal loss or technical issue. The projector then came on. This time it wasn't projecting the school's convocation ceremony theme nor the Chancellor who was on stage.

It projected me.

I looked up and saw it was me- I didn't understand what was going on until a video played. It was me in bed with Musa, naked while his face was blurred. It was projecting live on the screen; nearby was a national news outfit covering the event. I was dumbfounded. I didn't believe what I was seeing. I looked down and saw my mother, her mouth wide open, Maheer had backed the projector. Melinda was already on her feet. Mother looked at me, opened her mouth to talk but slumped instead. Maheer rushed to her likewise the others. I remember the disappointing look on the Chancellor's face as the award dropped from his hands. The other guests were giving disapproving looks. I wanted the earth to swallow me at that instance, and when I finally felt myself, I ran to my mother.

"Mummy! Please get up!"

"Get your hands off her, you whore!" Uncle Jimmy, who I didn't know was present, barked.

I was heartbroken. How did I go from the glorious child to a whore in seconds? It was a second strike, but I managed to put his harsh words aside and focus on my mother, Uncle Jimmy pushed me away.

"You are a disgrace to this family."

"Stay out of this Jimmy!" I retorted. I had never for once been a fan of his and wouldn't tolerate him, not this time. I could not afford to lose my only surviving parent.

"Mum, please. Don't leave me. Mom, open your eyes. Mom, please."

A great silence fell on the hall, and they watched us battle our shame. The emergency team came in. I tried to follow but was stopped when I got to the ambulance.

"We have had enough of you, sister. Please stay away from us," Maheer said with his back to me.

"How... But she's my mother too. I ... it was... Maheer..."

“Fareedah, stop! Don’t touch her. Get away from us,” he said as he pushed me away. This was a boy I had gotten into a big fight for; this was the brother I had lied countless times for; this was my first love, who I had watched over and protected right from infancy. I landed on my left arm and had an instant dislocation. But I didn’t feel the pain. I felt nothing. My only concern was my mother. I picked myself up again and chased the ambulance till I got tired.

I was lost. I didn't know where else to go. By now, I could feel the pain from my dislocated arm, but it didn't compare to what had just happened. I would rather take it over and over again if it would erase what just happened. I kept walking, but all around me, people stared in disbelief. I later got to know he hacked into my social and released the videos as well.

“Isn’t she that proud law student?”

“Ashawo five naira, Good for her.”

They could whisper for all I cared. It didn't matter. Nothing did, actually. I heard my name and knew it was Melinda.

“Ridah, please stop,” she said, running as fast as she could. She would run out of breath before she covered the distance between us. She was an asthmatic and couldn’t do anything strenuous. Soon, I arrived at a place where I couldn't hear my name, where no one knew my face, I arrived at the lagoon front. It was always soothing and beautiful, but today I was too troubled to see it. I approached the bars around the lagoon and crossed over them. I just wanted to be gone and buried beneath the waters; perhaps, it would wash this feeling away. And there, I let released my grip on the bars and dove into the lagoon.

A month later

The courtroom was filled with people. Outside were lots of spectators from all sects. The bloggers, TV reporters, and others who wanted to really know how things would end. The only familiar face was Melinda's. We sat beside each other, her hands in mine. If all had gone well, I should be in law school now, not in a courtroom yet. My certificate was suspended until the university had conducted a proper investigation on the whole issue. I thought about how this would change all that had happened. Would it make me the glorious child again? I didn't know yet.

"Barrister Agnes, my attorney," Melinda's mother introduced herself.

"I'm sorry I was late. You know how Lagos traffic is."

"Good morning, ma," Melinda greeted.

"Don't worry, Fareedah. We will get to the end of this. I'm with you one hundred percent."

I smiled a little just as the judge walked in.

"Court!" the clerk ordered. He read the case. The prosecutor, Barrister Mike proceeded. My mind wandered off to when it all began. Thomas had often told me Musa was bad luck to begin with. He was possessive and controlling. He suffered from abandonment issues and would do anything to have people stay in his life. I pitied him more than I loved him. His mother died due to domestic violence, and his father became a fugitive. He had to live from one relative to another with constant taunting from them and a reminder that his father killed his mother. It was right to say he was damaged, but I still wanted him. Although I was an academic year ahead of him, I didn't care. We began our romance when I was in my third year out of the necessity to heal from my father's demise.

"...In a country with cultural values and beliefs which lay emphasis on morality, it can be said that Ms Fareedah did place herself in the wrong position..."

"Objection, my Lord. My colleague is ..."

"Objection overruled. Please, proceed, Barrister Mike."

"What I was trying to get at was that Ms Fareedah compromised herself as well as her dignity as a woman and allowed for herself to be victimized. My client is equally a victim of this scandal. He has lost his job as a computer and data analyst at one of the top tech companies in the country. On this note, I would love to call on my client, Mr Musa Ahmed."

"Mr Musa Ahmed, please approach the court."

This was the first time I'd seen him in four months. Ever since the breakup, I had severed all ties with him. Just seeing his face made me sick to the stomach. I wanted to pounce on him and tear him into shreds. As if reading my mind, Melinda held my hand in hers till they pinched. By now, Musa had undertaken his oath, and I knew he was going to do the opposite. He didn't even believe in Allah.

"Mr Musa will you tell the court how you met Ms Fareedah."

"I met her in university during my sophomore year."

"How did you both begin your romantic affair?"

"My senior course mate, Thomas Philips, approached me one day and told me his female friend was into me. I thought he was kidding because she was so beautiful for me and a year ahead of me. I brushed it off, but he insisted that it was true. He then gave me her number.

"Do you know if Ms Fareedah had sent him?" Barr Mike asked

"Objection, my Lord, this question is of no relevance to this court. How two people met and their affair has nothing to do with the court."

"Barrister Mike, I see no relevance as well. What's the point?" Judge Martha Stewart asked.

"I'm sorry, your honour. I was trying to establish a point."

"So, after getting chatty with her, when and where did you meet officially?"

"Well, I can't say how long we chatted for because she was usually occupied, but it was after a while did we run into each other at a club."

What was he saying? What club? I have never been to a club. Even when Melinda had tried to get me to attend, I refused to.

"Did you both agree to meet at the club, or did you run into her?"

"My Lord, my learned colleague is misleading with his question."

"Overruled."

"Answer the question, Mr Musa."

"I ran into her there, and we just kept talking."

"Can you describe her composure and behaviour at the court?"

"Objection! This is of no relevance whatsoever."

"Let me rephrase that. When you met Ms Fareedah at the club, did she have the aura of a frequent clubber or a onetime attendee?"

"A club is usually a place one loosens up, so I can't really say, but she was free and seemed to have lots of friends there."

"It's a lie!" I shouted as tears dropped down my face.

"Miss Agnes, please restrain your client!" Judge Martha Stewart ordered.

"Relax, Ridah," Melinda said.

"How long did your relationship last?"

"A year."

"And what ended the affair? And who?"

"Cheating. She did."

I couldn't believe my ears. I never cheated on this psycho, not even when I saw him flirt with my coursemate, nor had another lady in his bed. I was with him through his STD's, and I only broke up with him when he attempted to rape me. How did I get into this? I have lost my family; my mother is still in coma, ever since the incident. My siblings would hate me forever should she die. And now, my five years of education was taking a trajectory down the drain. Why did I live? Why was I saved? Why did the Lord not take my life?

I remember the day I jumped into the lagoon. I didn't resist nor fight when the water began to fill my lungs. I let it all in till I couldn't feel. How I survived, I don't know. I just know I awoke in the boat of a fisherman. I didn't have to deal with judgements until I was taken to the hospital.

"Isn't that the law student whose sex tape is trending?" some nurses gossiped while I was just a few feet away.

"I heard her mother died immediately."

"It's better not to have a child than to have one like this."

"Ashawo oshi! Girls of nowadays. They can't wait. Always jumping like kangaroos."

I was enraged.

"I am the daughter you will never have, you gossip, and any child of yours is cursed," I barked. It took them by surprise. A 'whore' dares confront them when she should bury herself in shame. She should make herself invisible to all and sundry. It didn't turn out well, and I was discharged afterwards.

Melindah came for me. She was the only family I had left. When she came to pick me up from the hospital, she said the most beautiful thing I have ever heard.

"You are a woman. Your genitals do not define you, and you shouldn't allow a bastard do that either. You will come home with me, have a hot shower and head for the courtroom. He's got to pay."

"I'm scared. I just want this to go away. I just want

mum to wake up, and I just run away."

"The door is wide open. Why don't you run? I bet it with you. You won't last an hour running. Then, you'd ask yourself, where you are headed? And you'd see nothing but their nasty comments, unworthy definition of you. You would come to face with this guilt they forced down your throat, and you'd choke and die. Or you can get up and define who you are in clear terms and unapologetically. The choice is yours. Let me know when you've made it."

"I don't think I'm strong enough."

"You don't need to. You have to act. Think about your father. He wanted you to be the first lawyer in your family. Are you going to let a bastard's act of selfishness take that from you? You earned every award and honour that came your way except this. I have known you for four years now, and I know this is unfair."

The next day her mother flew in her friend and attorney, Barrister Agnes. She familiarized herself with me, and it aided my healing. But it was hard. The court of public opinion sentenced me over and over again. It took blogging away from me. My blog was full of filthy and harsh messages. My sister was constantly harassed and taunted in school and on the way. I was the talk of the town.

She's been sleeping with all lecturers. That's why she graduated best.

I read a comment from one of my coursemates, Andy. He was second best in the faculty but always bitter towards me. I never took him as a competition. Why did he say this? But, he wasn't the only coursemate with the opinion. A lot of them did, and that only mattered a few weeks ago. Now, I was out to have Musa pay for turning my day of joy to sadness, my mother's happiness to illness and my siblings' love to anguish. He'd pay for turning my father's desires to dust. I wish I could kill him.

I looked up and saw Barrister Agnes questioning Musa, and I felt a bit relieved. When it comes to principles of law and defence, I trust her wholeheartedly.

"Before you, your honour, is a message from Mr Musa's phone to Miss Fareedah's. He deleted it from his phone, but the technology experts were able to fish it out from her *Icloud*, which we all know, can always be traced. The message shows Mr Musa's intention to give my client a gift for her ceremony and a countdown. The message came in at exactly 10 a.m., and the countdown was for ten minutes, the exact time the video was released." Turning to Musa, my lawyer asked, "What gift did you intend to give to my client?"

"Objection, my client bought a necklace prior to the ceremony and here is the receipt from the store."

"If it was a necklace, you'd have had to give her after the ceremony, but you included in your message a countdown, and that ended exactly ten minutes after you sent that message. How do you explain that?"

"Well, it is not uncommon for people to use countdowns. I don't know how this is linked to me?"

"But you denied sending a message to her earlier, and you then admit to using a countdown."

"Objection, my colleague is manipulating my client. Clearly, all this is too hazy to process for him."

"Overruled."

"Proceed, Ms Agnes."

"Were you aware of the leaked tape before now?"

"No."

"Here is a screenshot of your WhatsApp message with your friend, Kayode, about how you would do Miss Fareedah 'dirty' and show him proof of banging her. Do you remember any of this?"

"Hmmm, well, I was only telling him of my intention but ..."

"Do you or do you not remember, Mr Musa."

"I do."

"Also, your honour, here is evidence of Mr Musa's video message to Mr Kayode on the 17th of February. Three days after, he was with my client. The video was obtained from Mr Kayode's WhatsApp backup. Mr Musa did send this tape to his friend before it was leaked on July 29th 2019."

"Mr Musa, if you weren't involved in this scandal, why then was your face blurred?"

"I... I don't know."

"It can be deduced that Mr Musa did not only film this without my client's consent but also released it on the said date. This has caused distress to not only my client but her family as well. I have no further questions, your honour, and I'd like to call on Miss

Fareedah."

"Miss Fareedah Femi, please come forward."

I arose and headed to the clerk. I took the oath, and the question began. Barrister Agnes' questions had been rehearsed beforehand, so it was easy. Then it was Barrister Mike's turn.

"Were you aware of the video before the day it was released?"

"No."

"But you, on the 1st of January, told my client in a message that you fantasized about watching your sex video."

"That was to answer the question he asked. We were playing a game, and he asked me what my nastiest fantasy was."

"Do you believe this video was done out of love to fulfil your desires?"

"No. He filmed it out of his own selfishness and without consent. By the end of January, we began to have issues when he tried having sex with me. I refused."

"Why?"

"Because he was treating gonorrhoea at that time. I knew he must have had other sexual partners. I was enraged and vowed never to have anything to do with him. That was the third STD he treated in two months."

"My client said he had caught you with several partners, and you infected him with these diseases."

"He's a liar! We have never had unprotected sex. I

always buy the condoms myself because he would want to use it as an excuse. In fact, I have a pharmacy where I buy it regularly."

There was murmuring in the court. How would a girl shamelessly buy condoms and still say it? I was done with their hypocrisy. Musa had admitted to bragging about sex, which was normal, like he had sex with a tree.

"Miss Fareedah, you and my client were seen hanging out on the 14th of February, a day for lovers. It's apparently the day the leaked video was filmed. What made you so sure that it was my client who did it?

"Musa is well known in that hotel. And that particular room has always been reserved for him. I was not happy with this fact, but he'd tell me he couldn't concentrate on work in his apartment which he shared with two of his friends, so he preferred the comfort of the hotel. This gives me the absolute conviction that he had been to the room ahead of time and set whatever cameras. Besides, the room key was with him on arrival. And the log from the hotel said he checked in alone at 3:00 p.m. The camera footage showed the same thing. We arrived there around 8:00 p.m."

"Ms Fareedah, you are being a lawyer here. And you aren't one yet."

"I was only stating the fact," I insisted. I would not allow a crooked lawyer to mask the truth with old tactics.

"I understand that seeing your video must have been

traumatic for you, but don't you think it might have been one of your numerous lovers."

"I'd like the prosecution to refrain from such insinuation as he has no proof whatsoever to support that claim."

"Mr Mike, do refrain from that statement."

"My apologies, your honour. Miss Fareedah, do you suspect that it was one of your acquaintances that set this up?"

"If it was one of my acquaintances, then there won't be WhatsApp exchanges between Kayode and Musa. Also, the message won't be sent to me at my convocation ceremony at the time I was about to be awarded. This was done by someone who knew the order of things. Musa was also a student of the institution."

"Thank you, Miss Fareedah. No further questions, your honour."

"Miss Agnes, any more witnesses?" Judge Martha Stewart asked.

"No, your honour."

"Mr Mike, any more witnesses?"

"No, your honour."

"Now, to the closing argument. Prosecution Counsel."

"The argument of the defence counsel rests on two things. One, the integrity of the accused as one of the top computer experts in the country. Even though we have had top officials become criminals. Two on the testimony of Mr Thomas, a friend of Miss Fareedah, who clearly seems hurt by the unreciprocated love, that indeed, my client was wayward. I am tempted to question what waywardness is. Is it a crime to be sexually active as a woman but as a man be given accolades? And since when did sexual activities justify collateral damages? It is Miss Fareedah's turn today, but it can be any woman tomorrow. This is not a crime against a woman or two. It is a crime against a community and womanhood at large. And this has to end. The double standards, the crucifixion and suppression of women, has to end right now, in this court. Miss Fareedah's mother has been in a coma for a month now. Miss Fareedah's five years of education is going down the drain all because of a man's ego. A man's inability to take no for an answer. A man's sense of entitlement to a woman's body, we shouldn't turn a blind eye to this. If we do, we do not only justify this act of selfishness but also leave our girls unprotected.

"The question remains, "why will a man of reputation stoop so low to banter and leak a video of himself with a woman? My client, Mr Musa, has clearly shown that he was indeed a faithful partner during the time of courtship, a fact Miss Fareedah testified. Why then will he hurt the one he loves? His level of expertise is questioned as well. Being a computer genius has been the primary base for these allegations. Is he wrong to have been so good at handling computers? Should he be put behind bars for being good at what he does? Are we going to kill a blossoming flower because the branch is crooked?" Barrister Mike concluded.

"Bringing this to an end, the court will allow the jury to deliberate before the verdict is given. The court hereby takes an hour break."

Barrister Agnes walked up to me after the judge had taken her leave.

"Miss Fareedah, whatever happens, justice will be served. Now, let's get something to eat."

As we stepped out of the court, journalists surrounded us immediately.

"Miss Fareedah, was it true that you consented to the video?"

"Is it true that your mother is dead?"

"Whether or not my client did consent, that is no justification for revenge porn. However, my client was a victim of his voyeurism as well as unauthorized access. We await the court verdict today, and I urge the members of the public to remain calm and refrain from false tales about my client. Thank you." With this, we went into Melinda's car and drove to a nearby restaurant. I was now comfortable to be seen in public. Forty-five minutes spent, in no time and we headed back to the court.

We settled in, and the court resumed session.

Judge Martha began. "The court hereby finds Mr Musa Ahmed guilty of voyeurism, revenge porn charge, as well as unauthorized access to a digital gadget in the fifth degree. The current state of Miss Fareedah's mother as well as the distress of Miss Fareedah cannot go unheard for it is the distress of a community and womanhood. This court hereby sentences Mr Musa to the maximum penalty of five years in Ikoyi prison, and compensation of five million naira be paid to Miss Fareedah. Also, the video be expunged from the internet. Officers, execute order!"

"Court!"

Melinda gave me with a knowing face. She has always been there for me. I couldn't have done it without her.

"What next?" she asked.

"I need to see my family."

Barrister Agnes approached us with a sad face.

What was wrong? At least he has been put behind bars.

"The university has reached its verdict. Your certificate has been withdrawn," Barrister Agnes said.

Strangely, I didn't panic. I smiled.

"Barrister Agnes, I think I will be needing your service once more, pro bono." I winked.

If was followed by an outburst of laughter from the three of us.

SEE

ENYI NNABUIHE

When the spirit of the Lord comes over Sade the first time, she is born again, but she is too young to understand what it means. She is riding back home in her father's Ford Escort when the golden yellow light penetrates her chest, diffusing love, joy and peace into her, flushing away the bitterness her teachers claim she'd displayed at her tender age. The gleaming goodness encompasses her at this instant before she can even take another breath. It takes only seven seconds for the chant spewing from her lips to be altered from Fela's *'Expensive Shit'* to a more heavenly language.

She may not understand what has descended on her, but she feels at home with it. She adores it. She remains calm and makes herself a vessel for this spirit to do as it wishes, but she terrifies her father in the process. Through the rear mirror, he peeps at his daughter but only sees her brown lips dancing sporadically to a rhythm he never taught her. He's befuddled. His fingers clawing at the steering wheel with fright and confusion, he watches her stare into nothingness, her *súkù* sticking out her occiput like one enormous bronze horn.

Something within him cautions him, telling him to

admit that this is beyond him, perhaps, even beyond Fela's therapeutic lyrics. But he increases the volume of the track, intensifying the trumpets and the raspy voice. He screams at the top of his lungs in imperfect harmony, "my shit na exhibit, it must not lost oh!"— words of revival he believes will deliver his daughter and reverse whatever nonsense is happening. He gives it seconds, waiting for her little voice to pick up with her singing, for everything to go back to normal, but sadly, nothing changes.

So, he turns off the car's ignition in the middle of the road, shuts his eyes, and as he does what he considers praying— Fela's irate singing still playing in the background, his darling Sade begins to tremble uncontrollably, spewing a foamy liquid now, and not gibberish words from her lips. It is at this moment it becomes certain that his gods have returned like they said they would, as they promised they would.

That night, after taking Sade to the hospital just to hear the nonsense the doctor will utter about a mild convulsive seizure that'd suddenly overcome her and how Phenobarbital plus a three-hour rest would do the trick, Mr Adelotan cleans out the room he's always told his wife to keep away from. He lays his daughter on the concreted floors and erects six candles about her like an anointed lamb— two by her head, feet, and at each side of her trunk. He listens silently as required for a successful ritual, but the distant muezzin call, an indistinguishable splash, whomp and thud as someone draws water from the neighbourhood well resounds in its absence. So, he makes do with what he has, focusing on the candles, gleaming as the flames burn brightly, bathing the unpainted room in its divine orange-yellow, yet casting thin, shackle-like shadows that ran along the floors, up the walls, across the ceiling, and around Sade's mollified body.

In chalk, he scribbles a vivid image of Yemoja, the deity after Sade; letting her fierce eyes and voluptuous entirety run from his little girl's bare chest to her gnarly hands and feet. He then kneels outside the altar he's consecrated and placed her in, his eyes set on the shadows and Yemoja's frightening image for a sign. He will sing for hours till she flees from his daughter's insides as wisps of smoke in the form sketched on her skin.

He claims he has the authority of Orunmila, toughening his voice, so it is livid and peevish like Fela's own, and he tells her to flee, that she has come far too early, and it is not yet his Sade's time. Over and over, he does this, night after night, till Sade sees the Lord a second time, three years later, rings of fire burning mightily around His waist.

It is a trance she is sent into after she listens to her mother's protruded belly and hits her head forcibly on the ground. He is more graphic and incandescent this time. Maybe she would even call him beautiful if her eyes could meet his eyes or nose or lips. He lends her a hand, and through its warmth, she tastes His kindness. He picks her up from the ground, lets her dust herself, and then shows her the so many times in the eleven years of her life she has not been patient. Like when her seven-year-old self bent a little boy's knuckles backwards after he'd stolen her crayon. Like when she was in primary four and started a fight with someone who had cut the queue. And like two weeks ago when Abraham, one idiot in her class, pulled up her skirt and sprinted.

She sees herself flare up and chase Abraham out of the class, down the hallway, to the parking lot at the back of the school. Abraham's agility is, to an extent, greater than hers. She scours for a hack on the ground to slow him down. She sights three rocks along the path and picks them up despite knowing her terrible aim.

She hurls.

One shatters the windscreen of the coaster bus and lands on the driver's cushion. One goes over the fence into another compound from where a woman screams:

"Ewoo, my flower pot!"

The last one hits Abraham, her target, at the back of his head, sending him to the ground with a wham.

In a matter of seconds, Abraham begins to bleed. Tears well up in his eyes as he places his hand where he feels the hurt, to feel the injury and see the blood. Tears roll down his cheeks as he watches Sade step closer to him, fists balled, teeth clenched, eyes deadened. A part of him wants to plead; a part of him wants to guffaw and call her a freak with huge *nyansh* like the headmistress' own, but he struggles with these two parts of him and keeps mum.

She sees herself grin at Abraham's broken and

defeated frame, at his crystal blue uniform shirt soaked in his tears and blood, at his palms put together vertically, in total submission to her. She picks up the rock that hit its target, smiles, and although the Lord doesn't show her slam it on the sides of his head more times than she can count, she hears it— the smashing, Abraham's irritatingly shrill screaming, everything. She hears the headmistress saying awful things about her, her mother scolding her in Yoruba, her father's feet tapping the floors tensely and arrhythmically. Then, everything fades to grey, and she is alone with Him again. No Abraham, no blood, no voices.

He glistens even more and is about to show her another moment when suddenly, she screams, propelling herself to a void where the white meets the grey but doesn't mix with it. He is there before her, beside her, and suddenly great confidence overwhelms her. She says, 'how is am I supposed to be patient when Abraham did that kind of thing to me? she asks if turning a blind eye would have made Him think better of her if that was what was expected of her. She tells him of boys like Abraham, who take timid and helpless girls for granted, and think they can do whatever they want because they are sure the girls won't retaliate and they'll get away with it. She asks him why he even let Abraham's parents name him Abraham if he knew he would be nothing like whom he was named after. She asks how Bible Abraham behaved as a child. If he was anything like stupid, dustbin Abraham in her school. His silence strikes her, so she asks how real He even is. How real the Bible is - if the characters were people who lived or pawns to stories that have been told too much, for too long, so they now seem real. She says she has one more question, then goes on her knees amid the void— its light and darkness— and says that He should please, please, answer this one, and with her vision clouded with tears and blinded by His magnificence, she asks Him if He created the world, then who created Him.

Tranquillity overcomes her thoughts, her mind, and her soul, but on the outside, her muscles are palpitating, and her mother is flailing her hands, running from parlour to room to balcony, panicking, and screaming, "Blood of Jesus, Baba Sade, Blood of Jesus!" She goes into labour at that moment, in that tension, so she keeps calling on the Lord, louder and louder with each pain she feels, till the baby, Ayanfeoluwanimi, begins to cry.

The years passing leave Sade distraught as she neither sees nor hears from the Lord. She feels, deep inside, that He deserted her because she didn't understand what He stood for and questioned Him only to nourish her disbelief in Him. She understands now how one's life could just be a series of meaningless encounters without Him, or like a thin piece of wool; lost, forsook, not tethered to anything. So, she tries many things to get herself to see Him again. She calls on Him by his many names— Jireh, Yahweh, Elohim, El Shaddai. She kneels, at night, her eyes closed, her hands put together, and she begs Him for His warm golden-yellow light one last time. Sometimes, she begs, pacing, crying, and trampling over her LAMLAD textbooks like she will not need them in April for Junior WAEC. Then, she gets a phone from her parents before SSS1 starts— this Nokia 3310 that only has Calculator, Torchlight, Phone, Contacts, a ridiculously addictive snake game, and 2go.

She meets someone on this 2go, someone who calls themself *Citizenofheaven2020*, who causes her to be more pleased and less disturbed. Someone who tells her she is not bonkers and actually makes her believe it. Someone who says they are just like her and have felt the Lord pass through them, but in a crimson-violet wave. Someone who tells her about the very few of them and their Facebook group but makes Sade guess what the last four numbers of their username stand for before she's added.

"I don't think I know," she says truthfully, and they inform her that it's the year of His second return, the year of rapture. He told me when He appeared to me, they say, and Sade, in utter amazement, becomes ensorceled by them, this genuinely ethereal *Citizenofheaven2020*. They chat about the Lord and their trances for hours, and Sade tells them that she wants to see Him again, that she's been trying, so they advise her to be more perfervid about her spirituality like it's the only task she was brought to this earth to accomplish, and she listens. She sends herself forth from the Sunday School to the Adult's Church. There, she learns to recite the Apostle's, Nicene, and St. Athanasius' Creeds by heart. She gets confirmed, and takes the sacrament of Holy Communion like it is her body she gobbles, and from her side, she gulps; hungrily, thirstily, sacredly.

She stops watching comedies and children's shows and starts being more involved in Nigeria— in the floods, the upcoming elections, and how it's already been more than a year since the Chibok girls were abducted. She doesn't want to think of them and the fact that they were just around her age or let her mind wander to the girl they buried alive because she refused to deny Jesus. But she questions herself immensely, for what would she have done had she been in the girl's shoes?

She cries, turns eighteen the next day, and declares that she's given up on ever seeing Him again.

The next Sunday's sermon, centred around Paul and Silas, gives her the idea of imprisoning herself in her room, so immediately after church, she does just that. She weeps behind closed doors, speaking to herself, telling herself things she feels He'd say at a time formidable as this. She eats the food Ayanfe passes under the door for her and drinks the water from the tap in her bathroom. She piles plastic plates by her bedside so mosquitoes can fly in and peck and peck and keep pecking `on the leftover grains and her flesh. Then, a brilliant plan takes form— fall ill, die, see Him.

While she plots and executes, her mother knocks, sobs, and on most days, falls asleep by the door, hopeful that by the morning, it'll be open. But Sade is so close to seeing Him again, she knows, so she doesn't cave to her mother's whimpering. She pleads, looks up to Him, and allows for the perching.

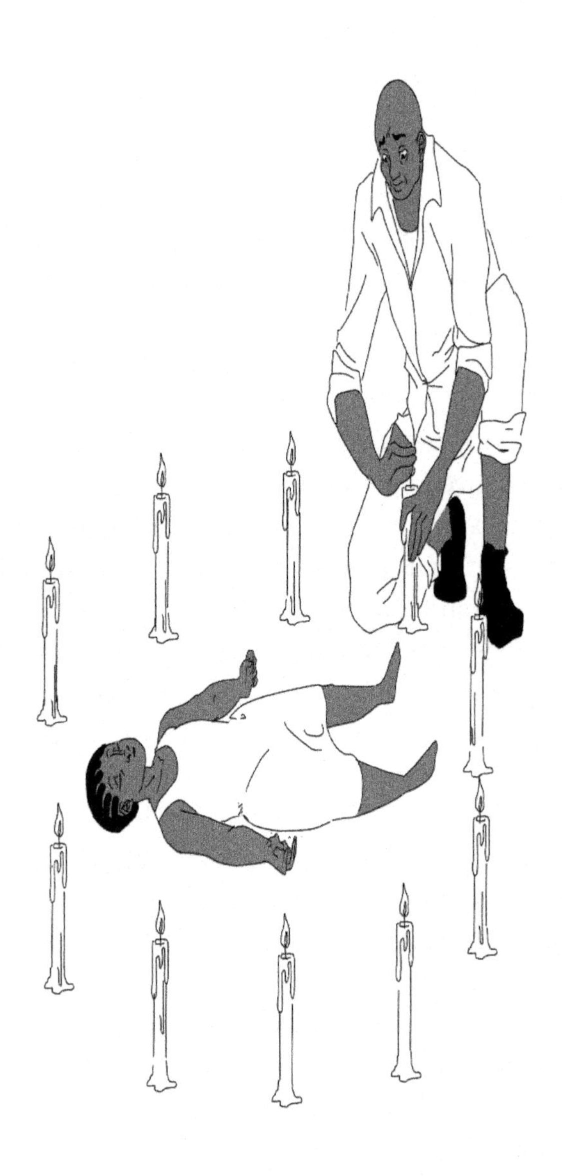

Then, one particular morning as Ayanfe slides a plate of macaroni and stew beneath her door; she obeys the something within her that tells her to step closer to the door and open it. She sees her little brother in his school uniform— white collared T-shirt, grey knickers, red tie with silver stripes— and grins widely. She remains by the door, but no words proceed from her parched lips. Her eyes move from his wrung mouth to the effulgence in his eyes, and as she's about to shout His names, burst into laughter at what He put her through, and embrace Him in Ayanfe, her mother appears at the space between the door and its frame. She pushes to keep the door open, and Sade pushes to close it.

"Sade, *ṣe o ya were*, you want to injure me?" her mother queries furiously, but with a wave of worry overshadowing it.

Sade puffs her cheeks as she pushes with all her might. "Màámi, I have to see Him."

"Folashade, *Ki lo fe*, see who?" She presses her cheek on the wooden door to support her hands. "Folashade, whatever it is, with the help of God, your father and I will help you get through it."

"It is Him I want to see."

"But you know your father is at work."

"No, not Bàámi," she replies.

"Who then, Sade?"

The door slams in her mother's face, but she keeps screaming. 'Who Sade? Sade, who?' till the time of twilight when her husband returns and talks her into sleeping in their bed, and not by Sade's door. This night, she waits for him to fall asleep, then she tiptoes to the door and sits there, crying and clutching her Bible to her bosom till she dozes off, leaving Sade to continue striding and receiving advice from her divine friend whom the Lord proclaimed His coming to.

It takes two months of no Holy Communion, a diagnosis of chronic malaria, and a dick pic from *Citizenofheaven2020* for her to pave the way for the realism that He's truly gone, that His heart has been hardened, that she shall not catch a glimpse of Him once more.

After recovering, she stands in front of the mirror and glares at her reflection; she concludes that she doesn't want to be this skinny, eye-bag-ridden religious fanatic anymore. So, before dinner, aiming to be unrecognisable, she snipes off her virgin hair with scissors and then uses Ayanfe's clipper to shave off surviving strands. She struts to the dining room, her shaven head dribbling water, and she announces her desire to change her name to something spicy, something sensual, something that screams, sings, and shits YOLO. Her parents don't know what to say or how to make sense of what she says, so they stare, and Ayanfe stares, too, at his sister's *gorimakpa* and the light bulb dangling from the ceiling directly above it.

The third time comes at a party on the west side of campus behind the Faculty of Law building. A friend invites her and gifts her a ticket, but on getting to the venue, she doesn't see the friend. Nonetheless, she decides to stay. She drinks stout, vodka in a little glassware, and stout again. Then, a little inebriated, she grabs a stranger by the round neck of his t-shirt, seduces him into buying her stout, and makes him rock her to the melody of Davido's *'If'* blasting from the speakers, just so she can size his penis.

Unlike the first time the Lord descended on her, she does understand what she's doing. Maybe she doesn't know why she's doing it, but every heartbeat seems to arouse everything in her. She turns her eyes to his, makes her way down his sleeves with her fingers, whispers in his ear a 'yes', and at the next blink finds them in a bathroom stall, moaning and cussing, all of her begin to pulsate. Twenty-five minutes later, after the murder of blitzed and jaded youth, she is in an ambulance headed to Wilton Hospital, Yaba, but within her, she sees Him, all of Him. Finally!

She wakes minutes later, a blurry, rackety fan overhead and her mother, dissevered by the bedside muttering words with her head on her lap. A smile creeps on her face when she notices her daughter's eyes are finally half-open, and intermittently, tears roll down her ruffled cheeks to her unctuous neck. She sights her daughter struggling to lean up, so she rushes to her side and assists her. She tells her to take it easy, puffs the pillow beneath her, then presses her lips against her forehead.

But Sade, with a drowsy composure, continues to struggle, so all of her back can lean on all of the hospital bed's white metal frame. Her eyes move from the window's view of the clamorous city streets to her mother's eyes, then to her arm. She sees a bandage and a narrow tube leading to where her eyes can't follow at the moment, and she screams as loud as she can, which is as loud as a tortured squirrel's squeak. With the little energy she has, she tries to rip the bandage and the tube, but her mother stops her and overpowers her.

She feels an additional weakening seeping into her bones, painfully, gallingly, making the feeling altogether dangerously pleasurable. It wraps around her like a rope, like the thin, untethered rope she is without the Lord. The Lord. Yes, the Lord! He came over her in the violently inspiriting way He usually does. He usurped her, and that's why she's here, on this bed, drifting out of unconsciousness and gradually, back into it. But she doesn't recall what He said to her, or what He showed her, or the calmness of his golden-yellow light.

She closes her eyes to remember, for she must remember, for how can she wait nine long years to see Him to not remember her encounter with Him? Her fingernails dig into the hibiscus-patterned bedsheets, claw at them, and tear, frustratingly.

She doesn't remember. She can't remember!

"Why can't I remember?" she screams, her voice finally finding itself.

"Remember what, Sade?"

"Him! I can't remember Him!" The tears overwhelm her now, and the crying breaks her voice into a rough groan, but she keeps speaking. "First, I can't see Him. Now, when I see Him, I can't remember seeing Him?"

Her mother's eyes peer at her intently, like she understands, or if she doesn't, like she wants to like she'll do everything in her power to. So, she cries some more, her head, with all its aches and worries, on her mother's bosom.

For a moment, there's sobbing, then silence, then her mother says she should eat something, that the doctor said she'll need something strong to eat—possibly *amala* or *eba* if she can swallow— after that dose of injection he gave…

"Injection? What injection?"

Sade, as quick as she can, gets away from her mother's face, away from the bed.

"Màámi, what was in the injection?"

Her mother says she doesn't know, then tells her to sit back down, that she may faint if she takes another step.

But Sade keeps limping backwards, yelling at her mother to stay away from her, screaming, "That's why! That's why I can't fucking see Him!"

Her mother steps closer, repeats herself, tells her to return to the bed that maybe it's even the injection that's making her shout nonsense.

She says she's not mad and that she's not crazy. She yells it so hard and so loud that her mother shrieks. She admits, in stutters, that she can see God, and that He sees her, and that He loves her! That He tells her things she should know to be better, that He teaches her how she can be an embodiment of Him, and only Him. That

He gives her peace!

She keeps talking, narrating her encounters with Him, but her mother, not understanding what she says, screams for the doctor and the nurses.

She gets on her knees and crawls to her mother. "You have to believe me! You have to understand that I have seen God." She holds the hem of her mother's gown and stares into her eyes for that warmth she saw earlier, for that peace, for Him, and as she does, a slim, bearded doctor rushes in with two nurses holding syringes.

They grab her by her arms to the hospital's profiling bed, and all she can see is her mother cupping her mouth in a fazed distance. She hears sobbing; hers, her mother's, and one that belongs to Ayanfe, who stands at the doorway, trembling. She hears the nurses complain about how her 'violent shaking will break the needle oh!' She hears the rackety fans, its screeching and swooshing, and it transports her to a divine trumpeting.

She hums to this celestial trumpeting, her eyes closed and mouth opened, as the doctor grips her palpitating wrist and floods her with this substance that will cleanse her of Him.

Forever.

RAIN, RAIN, GO AWAY

FAVOUR MARTINS

Aunty Ifeoma's madness came in bits and trickles. Like the water from the dysfunctional tap in front of my SS1 class. The water starts out fast and then reduces into a constant drizzle, leaving your hand dry like farmlands thirsty for rain.

She walked with a constant dip, an unwavering ecstatic grin and swept the house with the musky scent of her *Kente* wrapper and blouse.

Let me tell you the story that precedes this one. The story of how aunty Ifeoma saved our family. How she held the marriage of Daddy and Mummy together like a huge black pot on a tripod stand. Her capable hands had kneaded our family like dough into something between soft and firm - just the right consistency.

It had started that day she walked into our house. Aunty Ifeoma, our lord and saviour, radiant in her Ankara wrapper and puff-sleeve blouse. Mummy had brought her from Umuahia. She would be staying with us and cooking for us. I was a month away from twelve years old, and Naeto was just two years old. We stared at her with childlike wonder. Mummy had said she was bringing home a house girl, but it turns out she was a house-woman instead.

She had sat down on Daddy's couch, and we were all too stunned to tell her to move to another couch. Her aura was demeaning; she went into the kitchen like lightning and, in the shortest possible time, was out with the sweetest stew I have ever tasted.

When we sat at the dining table to eat later that night, Daddy had cleared his plate for the first time ever. He had requested for more, and Mummy rushed to the kitchen to dish out more of Aunty Ifeoma's delicious stew. It was an unsaid rule. Daddy could only know that Aunty Ifeoma guided Mummy in cooking the stew. But I knew. Naeto knew. The pots and pans that have been accustomed to the sour, watery taste of Mummy's stew knew. We all knew that Aunty Ifeoma was an angel. She had to have put something in that stew. Something that changed Daddy like magic. He never came home late again. He never exchanged words with mummy after dinner. He never skipped breakfast. He looked at Mummy as a golden pearl, his eyes glazed with heightened admiration.

What bothers me to this day is that Daddy acted like Aunty Ifeoma never existed. She tip-toed around him. When it was time for morning devotion, and their fingers grazed while trying to reach for a Bible, he cringed, and later he read the Bible with a fleeting expression. We did not talk about it. We never talk about things. That's why when Aunty Ifeoma started our night chats, I embraced it with the fervour of a man starved of food for a year.

It started the second night after Aunty Ifeoma came

to our house. Mummy told her to sleep in my room. She rolled out her mat and lay down on the pink Barbie carpet in my room. She folded some clothes into a pillowcase and placed her head on it. The first night, I slept without giving her even a glance.

That second night, the rains hit my windowpanes with an insane fury. The room was cold, and I curled up beneath my duvet. I couldn't sleep. I don't know what I was thinking about. I know that my eyelids couldn't find solace resting against each other. I stared at the white ceiling and breathed in the cool air adulterated with Aunty Ifeoma's musk.

"*Naetochukwu o na ehi ura na room mummy gi?*" Aunty Ifeoma asked.

Her voice was coarse, thick with an unmistakable Igbo accent.

"Hmmm?" I turned to face the floor, wondering why she was talking to me.

"*I naghi anu okwu Igbo?*" She asked with a slight sneer in her voice.

I didn't know how to tell her that I understood Igbo, but I couldn't speak it. I was better than all my classmates in school who were Igbo. Port Harcourt was a non-Igbo state, and I had lived there all my life!

"Chiokikedinma," she said.

I was shocked. Nobody had ever called me my full name in a long while.

She laughed with the ease of one who was used to startling people.

Why do you call our full names? I asked her, hoping she could understand English at least.

"What is Kike and Naeto? Overdiluted forms of a name that deserves to be owned and not ashamed of."

I was shocked. Her English was perfect! Slick, crisp, like the ten-naira notes Boma's father gave her for offering on Sundays. I remember how we would hoard all the crisp notes and give only squeezed tired notes because God could make them new if he wanted them badly.

Aunty Ifeoma was on her feet before I knew it. She was rummaging through her bag for something.

"Lemme show you something," she said in her *crisp-notes* English.

She brought out a book. "Shhh..." she whispered, pressing her index finger to her pursed lips. It was a brown leather book. The pages were brown, and the handwriting was beautiful. Cursive. Like the sweet smell of new clothes. The book smelt refreshing.

I looked at her quizzically, and she smiled. It was the most beautiful smile on God's circle earth. Her teeth dazzled; it was then I noticed how really beautiful she was. Pink small lips, a nose that stood like the London bridge rebuilt, surrounded by full cheeks and a mole above her upper lip. She looked younger than she did in her Ankara and puff blouses. Her nightie was a loose gown with a big bow tie at the lower trunk. It looked a bit childish for her age.

I read the first few lines of the book. 'Mary's journal', it said.

"My baptismal name is Mary," she mumbled as if reading my mind.

"Keep it. Read it later," she said as I tucked the journal into my school bag.

"Don't tell Mummy."

I knew what she meant. In my room, she would be Mary, the *crisp notes-English* lady. Outside, she would be Aunty Ifeoma. Mummy's house girl from Umuahia.

I went to sleep that night with questions in my mind.

Aunty Ifeoma from Umuahia could speak and write English? Wasn't she supposed to be a village woman?

Why did she come to our house anyway?

****

I'll tell you the rest of that story later. Or never.

Now, let's talk about Aunty Ifeoma's madness. I know you may think it's a metaphor - a representation of something else that happened, maybe. But honestly, Aunty Ifeoma was mad. Like the real pull-your-clothes, eat-dirt kind of madness. It still amazes me how a person could move from a sensible reality to an unconsciousness of sorts. How can you even explain that?

The first time, the madness came like a gentle wind, sweeping leaves, raising skirts. It raised our brows.

It was one of those Sunday afternoons when Mummy invited her friends from church for lunch. I still marvel at the utter hypocrisy of mummy's church friends licking aunty Ifeoma's stew over Bible study and complimenting mummy for learning so fast and cooking such amazing stew. I saw Mummy Belema snicker sometimes when mummy smiles and replies to all their compliments. But they do not tell her.

So, back to Aunty Ifeoma's madness, let me describe how the house looked when she started crying and tugging at her blouse zip and screaming obscenities in Igbo. It happened a few minutes past two pm.

I had turned thirteen. My pants had been drenched in red sticky fluid once and not again. It was the second term of JSS3. I was in the study helping Naeto with his colouring book while thinking of ironing my shirt for school. Mummy and her friends were laughing and talking loudly in the parlour. Aunty Adaora's laughter was the loudest, ringing from the parlour like thunder. Daddy was sleeping in his room.

The sun was at its brightest. My body itched and prickled from the heat. Naeto's bright purple crayon looked lilac in the study's dazzling white light. The fan blew hot air, and I was thinking of putting it off. Mummy screamed from the parlour. I stopped. Naeto was wide-eyed. I was out of the study in the next second. Aunty Ifeoma was sprawled on the lobby floor, half-naked. Tears hugged her cheeks, and her eyes were rolled back, revealing only a slight portion of her dark pupils and the white bulging ball. My heart skipped a beat. Her breasts were surprisingly firm and beautiful in their unclad glory. Her nipples were round and big. Darker than my tiny pink dots shooting out like ripe almonds. Her wrapper was tied loosely to her waist. The women were trying hard to hold her and cover her, but she fought tirelessly, like a wild beast. I watched in horror.

Daddy did not come out.

By evening, Aunty Ifeoma was calm. She woke up with a start and went about doing her work without saying anything.

Nobody talked to her about it. We never really talked about things.

That night, I looked up at the white ceiling in my room and listened to Aunty Ifeoma's soft snores. I wondered how a person could walk into and out of madness like through a door, unafraid, unperturbed. There was something about Aunty Ifeoma that was unsettling. Something I couldn't ever place my fingers on.

****

The second time Aunty Ifeoma's madness came, it was a calm undoing. Like loosening a tied shoelace, dragging one lace to free the other. It came in the morning. Like it wanted to be greeted with the day. It slipped into the cracks that had been slowly forming in our home since the first time it came. Aunty Ifeoma was bathing Naeto, and then she began to sing. A melodious song. Her voice was a sweet, melting ice cream, shrill, cold, piercing.

As she sang, she covered her face with the lather from Naeto's bathing sponge and sat on the wet bathroom floor, smiling brightly. When Mummy came into the bathroom, Aunty Ifeoma pointed at Naeto and laughed. A beautiful, lathered woman, laughing hysterically.

Naeto was crying, Aunty was singing, and the sound of Mummy's heart drumming against the walls of her chest was deafening. The sound of water pouring from the shower was diminished in the light of all the human sounds. I helped Mummy carry her up to my room. We tucked her in and allowed her to sleep.

That night, Mummy cooked her watery bitter leaf soup, and we all ate in silence. Aunty Ifeoma slept on my bed that night.

The cracks were deepening and deepening. There was a deep foreboding lurking around the rooms and concrete walls.

That night, I read her journal while lying on her mat. I read five pages.

She wrote letters to God.

I read every single one of them, and then I began to feel guilty for listening in on her personal prayers. I wondered if Aunty Ifeoma really loved God that much or if he was just a fail-safe way of pouring out her heart to an unnamed individual.

The letters would start with 'Dear God', and end with 'Your Mary'.

They were mostly full of questions and uncertainty and something I perceived as desperation.

I remember one paragraph. I had read it three times and copied it into my Basic Science notebook. It embodied some of the questions in my head.

"What is a person living in the vast nothingness of

time? What is school and God and love and hate? What is a life that rests on the thin lines of death? Grief. Loss. What is a person with no future?"

It's funny how she asked 'What is God?' in a letter to God. I wondered why her letters were so pessimistic. Quite a paradox!

Her unwavering grin was a huge contrast to her letters.

She never talked to me about her journal during our night chats. She would talk about school and ask if I liked any boys, or girls. She slapped my small breasts sometimes and said they were growing slowly. She said that when my breasts itched or pained, they were growing. She washed my pants by herself the day I found them bloodied. She said I was now a woman. She said I had to smile and walk with my head straight and use pads. She told me it was normal when the blood didn't come again till I was fourteen.

Whenever I asked about anything in the journal, she would smile and say she couldn't remember since it was such a long time ago she wrote them. She didn't even tell me how long ago.

Sometimes she told me stories; of old times when just one naira was her pocket money for school, when girls didn't put on trousers and their skirts gracefully tapered at their shins when relaxers were trending, and girls were ashamed to carry nappy hair, she said that her relaxed hair used to get to her back, just above her bra strap. And people used to touch it and marvel at the smooth, untangling texture.

She told me about women that got pregnant before they were married and how they were scorned. She shook her head.

"I never understood why it was such a bad thing!" she said.

"How do people get pregnant?" I asked in return, and she smiled.

She said she would tell me when I was sixteen when Mummy allowed me to have a boyfriend.

Sometimes, Aunty Ifeoma taught me how to cook. I would boil rice, and she'd make the stew. She told me to put hot water in the bowl first before I spread garri evenly. She allowed me to grate the carrots and cut the peas for our salad.

Naeto called her, 'Aunty Toma' and we laughed. Naeto was three and could spell his name.

Aunty Ifeoma stayed with Naeto and me in the children's department in church and bought ice cream for us while we waited for the adult church to be over.

****

I remember the first time I saw the name in Aunty Ifeoma's journal. It was written in the finest handwriting ever. It was bordered by blotched paper, like three drops of tears had crystallized like wreaths around the casket on which the name lay, right there on her brown book.

I had asked her that night because I wanted to be sure that the Ikenna in Aunty Ifeoma's journal was different from Daddy's. We didn't answer Daddy's name in school. Our surname was his father's name. Obinwego.

"Who's Ikenna?" I tried to hide any form of curiosity. It sounded as casual as asking for a cup of water. But I could feel the tension the question had birthed.

When she opened her mouth to speak, I could tell that a story had slapped itself hard on her tongue, and she was trying to swallow it, to mortify it.

Her answer was simple.

"Have you ever wanted bread so much that when it is forcefully snatched away from you, you hold the crumbs and chew them eternally? Until your tongue is sore and bereft and bitterly wounded."

She chuckled.

I never understood her answer. But I figured it was better not to ask further.

I guess some things are not supposed to be understood.

Like all the never-delivered letters to Ikenna tucked away in her journal

One-word letters. *Come*

****

The third time Aunty Ifeoma's madness sat on our couch and ate our egusi soup, Naeto tore a page of Aunty Ifeoma's journal.

It happened so quickly, like light dispelling darkness.

I was carrying Naeto on my hip and reading the part in her journal about a story she had read. It's funny how she wrote a story about reading a story, and I'm writing about reading her story. What do you call it when there's an endless cycle of similar events?

Anyways, Naeto was giggling and digging his fingers into my hair. The sensation of the slight pull on the roots of my hair was a bittersweet accompaniment to Aunty Ifeoma's story.

I didn't know when Naeto's swift fingers moved from my hair to the brown pages of the journal, and the yanking was stronger this time. A ripping-apart. I screamed, and Aunty Ifeoma came running to the parlour.

"Naeto emebigo ihe! Naeto has destroyed my book o!" It was a soft, inside scream, but she didn't want to scold Naeto, who was curled up on the floor crying and muttering, "sorry, sorry" while still holding the yanked pages in his hand. His 'sorry' sounded more like 'soyi', and he looked so small at that moment. When I turned to look at Aunty Ifeoma, she blinked and walked back to the kitchen, where her pot of egusi soup was almost burning.

Mummy was not around. Daddy was locked up in the study as he always did when mummy wasn't around.

I went to the kitchen to apologize, and that was when I saw it. Calm, cold, sprawled on the cold tiles holding Aunty Ifeoma in her hands. Her sweet-looking face distorted in a weird smirk. Her eyes glistened with tears. I knew. I knew it had come again.

I ran to fetch Daddy, but he didn't come. When I opened his study, I saw him crying. An unusual sight.

Daddy was crying hard, silently, his shoulders heaving. I still wonder why to this day.

"Daddy, Aunty Ifeoma is acting unwell."

"I know," was his cold answer.

I stood staring at his back for a while and then at the books lined on the shelf. Many titles of rubbish books, a shield for crying souls. One caught my attention. The title was familiar: 'Sweet colours'. I couldn't place a finger on where I had heard the title. I peeled my eyes off the shelf and looked at Daddy again. This time he seemed small, like crying Naeto. The world was already getting blurry.

When I went back to the kitchen, It was empty. All that was left behind was the sweet aroma of Aunty Ifeoma's egusi soup. Every other thing was normal. Nothing had been tampered with.

Her clothes, her journal, her mat, her musky smell, the memories of deliciously cooked meals.

They all remained after she left.

****

Some things are still difficult to understand.

Like Aunty Ifeoma's smile and radiance amidst the rubble at the refuse dump at Rukpokwu. That day, she stood in glorious beauty. Like she had just emerged from a rebirth. Her hair had grown to a tangled halo, her now-black skin tapered at her core where overgrown, black dusty hair laced her V-shaped feminine glory. Her breasts stood firmer than ever. In defiance of nature's gravity. A testament of untouched femininity, the pride of pristine innocence. Her slender legs and bare feet were shiny black. She stood like a princess amid dirt and squalor. Ruling over her kingdom, doing as she pleased. Beautiful artwork! On her neck, a chain of old malt cans tied with a string, like gold on a queen.

I was in the car with Daddy and Mummy, and Naeto. Daddy froze the car as soon as we saw her. It was the first time we had seen her since she left. I was almost fifteen. Naeto was five. Our worlds had once again been condensed to the unkneaded dough that it was before Aunty Ifeoma.

I looked at her again. Her skin a resplendent onyx under the bright sun. Before she turned her back, I saw her smile. At something behind her. Or someone. A man clad with nothing as she was. It was the most beautiful smile I had ever seen. Her teeth still shone as ever.

When she turned her back, I caught a glimpse of her buttocks before Daddy drove the car away. Firm. Dark. There was a large, faint scar just below her left buttock. I wondered if she wrote about the scar in her journal. I had stopped reading it since she left.

I thought I saw a tear in Daddy's eyes as he drove the car away. Nobody talked.

That night, I picked up her journal from inside my wardrobe.

I opened the book with shaky hands and building tears. The pages that Naeto had torn out were tucked inside the book. I saw the story. The one I was reading the day Naeto tore the book. I saw the title of the story she wrote about; 'Sweet colours' - the same book on Daddy's shelf.

Naeto cried that night.

Nobody carried or cuddled him.

****

That night, I had a dream. Or maybe a memory painting itself again on my mind's canvas. Memories of the times before Aunty Ifeoma's rebirth. One of those evenings when the wind threatened to sweep the whole earth away. And trees swayed and danced, and clothes fell off lines. Aunty Ifeoma and I were hurrying to bring in our dry clothes before the rains descended heavily on them.

Naeto was giggling and running after us and singing *'Rain Rain go away, Come again another day...'* I joined him as we ran around, pulling clothes from the hanging lines behind our house. Aunty Ifeoma joined too. The chorus was loud amidst the thunder and wind.

Rain Rain go away
Come again another day
Little children want to play...

The world was beautiful before the cracks came.

ONYEKA: REBIRTH

CHIOMA OTTA

I died last night.

I kicked the bucket in my sleep, which was quite surprising to me because I had my life ahead of me. That night I was studying a script for a role I had secured after an audition. The next day, I was supposed to display my full-born acting talent. My utmost passion ignited after practically reading and digesting my part in the script. I remember acting out the role alone in my bedroom – a classroom teacher having a dialogue with the smartest student in her class. I was supposed to act as the teacher. But to my utmost shock, I woke up bodiless.

If I remember clearly, I witnessed my final moments at the hospital. I can still hear the faint sobbing and groaning in my household. My mother's wail was the loudest. She couldn't be consoled easily. I never knew she could cry like that. I had never seen her cry. She would quickly dry her tears on days when I caught her sobbing alone. Maybe because I was her first daughter, she expected me to live up to her shattered dreams. She always mentioned that her innocence was rudely taken away from her when she married my father. Was I to blame for her decisions? I will never know.

Father took the news of my death with more strength than I expected. He had always been the one to scold and criticize me on literally everything I did. Nothing I did was ever too good or too bad. It was just not enough for him. I guess he was relieved of that frustration now. I bet he would talk less, focus his energy on things that really matter or maybe start picking on my younger brother.

Brother was quite courageous. This I noticed when he scooped my body in his strong arms. I never knew he possessed such extraordinary strength in those teenage muscular arms. He was three years younger than me. He would never shed a tear. He should never appear weak because he was a man, but I could hear his heartbeat yearning for me to come back.

'Come back?

Not yet.

This other side felt magnificently incredible.

Sitting on a broken wall at the busy sides of the cemetery, the world felt anew. I can say it is more black and white than coloured. For example, when I was alive, the bright blue sky accompanied with a tint of yellow sun meant the day was going to be sunny. A grey sky with thick white clouds meant it was going to rain. Over here, the skies were greyer, ashen, and unpredictable. A grey sky was all there was, and I loved it.

I love the fact that I couldn't guess if the day would be rainy or sunny, winter or summer. I didn't care one bit. I was still navigating my newly found *grey* world.

I stared at my grave for days and probably months after my body was placed in that rectangular box, eagerly hoping there would be a miracle and somehow my body would float out from the ground, then I would return to the realms of colour – the land of the living.

However, that seemed irrelevant. I could not continue to wait. I never believed in either magic or miracle when I was alive. I believed things happened to people out of sheer luck or hard work. Right now, magic may not be possible, but I yearned for a miracle. It seemed everything I did not believe in was suddenly becoming the ray of hope for surviving in this grey world.

Staring and staring into the void, I see many faces - the face of a child, a woman, a man, the not-so-young man, the not-so-old woman - all present, alive, moving, chasing their reality like broken clay pot whose shards would never be pieced together no matter how much they tried.

Look at me. I died.

There is absolutely nothing to be afraid of.

I stare and stare at people from the coloured world come to visit their long-dead acquaintances or family. It seems every day was a death anniversary of some sort. I watched as couples trooped to mourn their child - children came to mourn their parents - colleagues came to mourn their partners. It was one huge, unending cycle.

My death anniversary was still far off. I wondered if

my family remembered me at all. I pondered at the thought. It was rather getting difficult to place their faces or remember their names at this point. I had no memory of how I looked anymore. But I knew there used to be a family where I came from else; I wouldn't be here in the first place.

They should be here anytime soon. Or probably they came, but I was too occupied in my own thoughts I did not even notice.

Was I losing sense of time too?

The *grey* world would bear me witness that I waited yet again.

Speaking about time – It sounded a little familiar. The *grey* skies hide the clues and signs of what time should be. What can I say? My biological clock ended the day I died.

Time was grey here - infinite, substantial, expensive. Ponder about time, and it surely leaves a bland taste in your mouth. Can I remember what month, year, and time I exited the coloured world?

No.

Was it today?

Today is not completely today. Tonight is not completely tonight. But it is wonderful there are no deadlines to meet over here. I have been basking in my own entity, watching rain droplets seep through my porous form and patiently witnessing the whoosh of the dark, wicked wind come to dry them off again.

The only closest word to describe the concept of time in this *grey* world is *again*. Things happen again and again over here.

No pun intended.

Just like an observer from another country who is permitted to peep in for a moment from the vast outdoors of freedom, I see the man at a distance. This figure of a man always took off his shoes as he approached as if there was a foot mat stamped at the edge of my grave. He would kneel in front of the grave in solitary, for hours offering food adulations. He made sure to clean up the area before leaving.

The remnant of energy left in me longed for human contact. So, I tried to communicate. It was as though I had a mouth filled with mumblings and incomprehensible musings. I opened my mouth once, but words failed. I knew I had such ability before, but it somehow vanished.

Our energies seemed to coincide. I felt like he adored this dead person, but whoever they were, did not matter in the grey world. I watched him leave just as he came. Now I have to wait again before I can see him.

Again.

When it rained, grey waters seeped through my form like I was made of small pores. When the sun shone, the rays warmed my very being, and when the wind blew, I felt a touch of weightlessness. I could float in the air. These were new to me at the same time; I felt like I had lived here forever. My knowledge of the grey world gradually broadened. I could manipulate the elements at will. I pretty much got attached to the wind. It could read my emotions. It felt like magic. I became powerful.

Into the void, I stare. I see the face of a woman and a little boy by the grave of her lost daughter. I allowed the wind to permeate my form, and I circled my grave seven times. It was a brave thing to do for the entertainment, of course. From a distance, a little boy tugged at the woman's clothes and pointed in my direction. My eyes widened, and I grinned.

Did he notice me? Did he see me?

I stopped circling my grave and stared back at him. Can he actually see me? I kept wondering.

The boy stands quite still, silent or at most uttering a brief human grunt as he waits for the spasm to pass. He turned away and began to cry uncontrollably. The woman understood the message. Before I could get closer to the boy, the woman whisked the boy in her arms, and they left hurriedly.

The heartbreakingly insecure snugness of these little humans. How entertaining!

I was one who never did care about looks. Maybe my nudity is a bit old-fashioned in the grey world. I should go back to my house and pick a cloth. Just suppose that the dead do revisit the living.

Would it even be worthwhile?

At best, surely, it would be like the brief visit of an observer from another realm. I made up my mind to visit my family.

I remember.

My favourite piece of clothing was the black

graduation gown my other had bought for me with her savings. I hope it still fits though.

Again.

I trudged home. It was a long, dreadful walk, but I was there just in time. The living room was dark except for the blue rays flickering from the television set. There was the bookshelf leaning against the wall opposite the window. These books have not made my father a scholar or, more truly, wise. It is just that he found a sense of accomplishment in acquiring more books. He misuses them quite ruthlessly - like when he needed to drown himself with philosophical words, which he threw back at me during his moments of fit and fury. I stare as he takes one of them down and strides to his bedroom. I sigh. I do not know what the man looks like anymore. I definitely was not bothered.

I came with the wind.

I felt powerful.

I passed by the windows, and they slammed shut. Brother walked to the window and looked up to the dark, coloured sky.

"It's going to rain," he announced.

It was not the rain.

I came visiting.

He shut the windows because he was afraid of the wind.

I am the wind.

Oh brother. You have no idea.

I walked to my bedroom window. There was the woman who birthed me in the coloured world.

I remember her.

I gazed at her closely. She lost a lot of weight. I placed the back of my hand on her neck. She twitched. Warm blood permeated through her veins. I picked up the blanket and covered up her body. All I could say or wish was, hurry.

Look at me. I died.

There is absolutely nothing to be afraid of.

I heard the man talking on the phone. I was not interested. Surprisingly everything here felt strange. Nothing seems to interest me anymore. I just wanted to pick up my stuff and leave. I did not want to feel the soil on my feet. It irritated me.

I witnessed the orange sunset with regrets. The dark blue skies were overwhelming.

I miss my grey world.

My utopian dream world is where I die to live.

I checked my little closet for my graduation gown, but I saw a vacant closet. Mother and her endless charity work. Where had she taken my priceless gown and my other clothes? This was so unbelievable.

The wind grew wilder.

I will have her gown until I find mine before I give it back. She had lots of favourites. I picked her a white blouse and a black flowing skirt; the one she wore on some Sundays. It was oversized, but I loved it. I heard footsteps – my brother walking down the corridor, heading to his room.

Brother must have felt my presence. He stopped walking and peered into my room. I smiled.

You can see me. Now you cannot.

The wind was so strong it knocked down the photo on the wall and slammed the windows against its railings. Brother was in my room. He replaced my photo frame on the blunt nail. My mother still slept peacefully. I took my leave through my bedroom window.

I was out now, in my grey, grey world. I took a shortcut and reached the graveyard. I returned to my sitting position, feeling proud of my new outfit.

The man came.

Again.

I was unusually thrilled to see him. He performed the usual food sacrifices. I stood beside him while he muttered words with his eyes shut. I remember I used to do that too, but now I had no idea what it meant.

It got a little windy. I did not want the wind to blow his flowers away. He opened his eyes and looked in my direction. I jerked back slowly when his eyes met mine. Can he see me?

"Am I obstructing your way?" he asked.

Wait. He can see my new form.

"Are you here to see someone?" he asked again. he sat comfortably in the grass and crossed his legs.

"You can have some food. It used to be her favourite." he offered me the crunchy brown piece.

He was speaking in words that came to me like muffled sounds. I gathered energy from the wind, and tapped my chest.

"Onyeka."

The words must have been conjured up from dark realms of my being because my throat collapsed.

He heaved a deep breath. "I am sorry about your loss. Onyeka. I know what it feels like to lose a loved one."

I shook my head and nodded at the same time.

What did he mean?

"I will be heading back." I watched him pack up the plates and spoons in a small basket. When he started walking, I followed a few steps behind.

"Are you heading my way?" he gestured.

He was quiet throughout the walk. His eyes must have seen a thousand sorrows. He took a detour towards a street. I followed him into his coloured world. I really wanted to say something, but I was literally lost for words.

"Are you going my way?"

I think he said that before. I tilted my head to make a response. It was already getting dark, and the streets were lonely. He remained quiet until we reached a line of small self-contained houses down a small street. I had never been to this part of town when I was alive. I followed him to the house. He turned around.

"This is where I live." He unlocked the door and stepped in. He tapped a switch on the wall, and a bright white came on, illuminating the room. I cringed as my form dissipated into the white rays.

I looked around the room. There were several family photos hung on the wall. You could barely see the colour of the wall.

"I lost my wife ten years ago. She was my best friend." The man said. " She left me to raise two kids alone. That is my first daughter. She loves football," he forced a smile. "And my second daughter, she wants to be a singer. She is also a good actress."

He pointed to a separate but distinct photo on the wall. "This picture was taken immediately after her heart transplant surgery.

My eyes followed the direction of his fingers. There was a framed photo of his second daughter. Bright smile. Wide-eyed. Glowing brown skin. She had a deathly gaze in her hollow eyes, just like me.

A heart surgery? Was that how my body was in the coloured world?

"She celebrated her sixteenth birthday in the hospital. She left for the university now."

What was he saying? I see only one thing in the photo.

My gown.

I gathered energy as much as I could and managed to lift my left hand. My index finger is pointing at the frame.

"Onyeka's gown."

"Oh, that gown." The man crossed his hands over his chest. "She got it as a gift from a kind woman who offered to donate her daughter's heart so that..." he sobbed, pinched his nose and breathed. "So that my daughter could live."

Mother gave her my graduation gown.

And my heart.

It got windy in the room, and the light went off. Before the man could turn it back on, I was gone.

Gone from the house. Just in time before the wind blew it off its foundations. I got teary not because of the gown but for no reason at all. There was no tear duct where tears could flow, nor a *heart* to interpret how I felt. So, I fought and clawed and gnashed my teeth.

I walked back to the graveyard.

Even if my form needed no heart to function, I still wanted my gown.

While I bask in the greyness of my world, I remember the girl whose heart beats in the coloured.

My heart. Her world.

My heart. Her life.

She holds my heart. I hold her life

Since I had already met her father, maybe I would give her a visit. Would it even be worthwhile?

Who knows?

Chioma Otta is a microbiologist, fitness coach, writer. She writes thrillers, drama and fantasy stories and has spent the last few years as a professional beta-reader. She hopes to finish her high fantasy trilogy book soon. She lives with her family in Aba, Abia State.

BLACK AND BLUE

WINNIE ENUNOSOWO EKA-WILLIAMS

Saturdays were the only days I could rest. Life as a lawyer fresh out of law school was as hectic as it could get, from competing with other lawyers in the firm I worked for a sit at the grownup's table to trying to balance work life with social life. Saturdays were created for me to take time for myself and do what I enjoy, and that was why I found myself in a bookstore every Saturday looking through various books and trying to decide which I was going to read. I was a regular at the bookstore, I knew all the workers, and the security man always cajoled me into giving him something every time I visited.

The Saturday I met Michael, I was wearing a blue chiffon top, my favourite everyday black jean and brown leather slippers with my tote bag, it was a rainy day, and I was thankful I was already inside the store before the clouds gathered. I had forgotten my glasses, and I thought it was a bad omen because who forgets their glasses when they're going to a bookstore.

The store was quiet. Some people were on their laptops in the lounge area, while some were at the cafe helping their selves to a cup of coffee. I didn't have a particular book on my mind, so I was glancing through and reading the synopsis and just judging them by their covers as I always do; I could never buy a book whose cover wasn't aesthetically pleasing to my eye. I had picked up a novel when the door opened, and there he was; he stood there in his six-inches glory, with a full face of beard and gold-rimmed glasses, the scent of the whole store changed, and his strong musky scent filled the space, he smelt like fresh wood and clean glass-very distinct description, I know.

I quickly looked back into my book and continued to read. I felt his presence as he moved around the store, with his head showing at the top of every shelf of the row he walked due to his height. I had read the synopsis of the book I was holding at least three times without remembering to understand what I was reading. I walked around more and took another book, and turned the back. It was a good story. I had finally found the book to get when I heard it.

"He dies at the end, and she goes off with her first love."

I whipped my head so fast I was pretty sure I must've cracked a bone; the book fell out of my hand. We bent together to pick it up and bumped into each other; this was so cliché. I was embarrassed at myself. He picked up the book while I held my forehead and got up slowly. We stared at each other and then burst into laughter.

"I'm so sorry," he finally said when he had stopped laughing, adjusted himself and looked at me.

"For breaking my head or spoiling my book," I

replied.

He offered to pay for my book, but I refused. He asked if he could get me a cup of coffee, and I obliged, we sat opposite each other beside the large window while we waited for our coffee, and I began to read the book I had paid for while he just looked at me, I could feel his eyes on my face, but I resisted the urge to look back at him and pretended to be completely indulged in my book, but I just could not take it, I set my book down calmly and looked at him.

"Did the bump leave a scar on my face?" I asked

"What? Oh no, there's nothing on your face apart from beauty," he replied and showed off his perfect set of white teeth.

I rolled my eyes and smiled a little. "Okay, good, because I'm a lawyer, and I can sue you," I added.

"Oh really? Wow! We would not want that; I have actually been looking for a good law firm to handle my company's legal needs. Do you work at anyone?"

"Yes. I'm a junior associate for Asuquo & Asuquo."

"I've heard about them; they were on my list, actually. If I employ the services of your firm, promise me you won't sue me?"

"I promise; I giggled and took a sip of my coffee. People really do find love in the strangest places, I entered my house, and my mom was seated watching zee world. She watched nothing else and knew all the Indian songs they played. She glanced at me.

"Madam, namaste," I mumbled, held back my laughter, and added, "Good evening, mummy." I handed her the bag of banana and groundnut I bought for her.

"Every time you'll be bringing fruits, when will you bring your husband, Anne?"

I knew where this conversation was going and rolled my eyes.

"You'll be 30 this year and still no sign of boyfriend, talk less of man that will marry you."

She went on and on while taking breaks to munch on the banana I brought for her. She went on and on, and I just sat there looking at her.

I didn't blame her. She wanted to see her daughter married like any other mother. I have two sisters, and they're both married despite my being the eldest. Law school was hard, I did not have any time for myself, speaking even more for another person, and I never really found the one. When I told the men that approached me that I was keeping myself for marriage, they'd always responded that they knew my type and tried to persuade me against my better judgement. The only boy I had dated was in NYSC. His name was Timi. I was so sure that he was going to propose to me when we returned home and he invited me to dinner. Apparently, he wanted to break up with me because he had just got married the previous Saturday. From then I did not bother anymore. I went about my life and only experienced love in the fake scenarios I created in my head and the happy ever afters I read in novels; that was enough romance for me. I could not sleep, Michael had dropped me in front of my house and did not bother asking for my number, and I could not stop thinking about what the reason might be. I decided to push the thought aside and go to bed.

The weekend went by in a flash, the much-dreaded Monday had come, and I had a case in court which was a very stressful process. I returned to the office past three, almost closing time, and I had to report to my principal before going home.

I knocked on his door and dragged my skirt further before opening it. Mr Okafor was a weird man. His eyes always lingered in places they were not needed, and his hands liked to follow suit; I always left his door wide open when I was in his office and tried to keep a safe distance. I walked in, and immediately, it hit me – I knew this scent from somewhere; the man sitting opposite Mr Okafor turned, and there he was. Michael. He offered me a small smile.

"Oh, Miss Anne, I was just about to send for you. How did it go in court today?"

"It was fine, sir. The case was adjourned to next month," Mr Okafor nodded.

"This is Mr Michael Orji. He is the CEO of MO Breweries, and He is our newest client," Mr Okafor said. "He wants you to personally handle all the legal matters of his company."

I was beyond shocked; this was a big elevation from my position as a junior associate. I had to contain my joy. I smiled and thanked him, he offered to drive me home, and I agreed.

"I'm sorry if I put you on the spot," Michael murmured as he opened the passenger seat, and I got in before he went round to the driver's side.

"It is really fine. If anything, I'm very excited and grateful to you."

We spoke about our jobs and the company and what I was required to do. He mentioned that they had an annual award ceremony. He would really like for me to come, I wanted to, but it was a Sunday. I absolutely dreaded leaving my room on Sundays, I did church online for a reason, I said I was going to think about it, and he accepted.

We got to my house, and I dropped out, he still had not asked for my number, and that made me sad, but I pushed it aside and thanked him before stepping out of his car.

My phone beeped soon after I got out of the bathroom. I dove onto my bed to get it expecting a message from Michael. I was so pissed when I saw that it was a message from Airtel. I threw the phone back on the bed. What was I even thinking? He did not ask for my number after meeting me again. I hated mixed signals. Maybe he was leaning towards a platonic friendship? But friends have each other's numbers. Even enemies have each other's numbers, so what exactly was going on?

I went on Instagram and searched his full name, and lots of Michael Orji's popped out. I put on my FBI cap and started eliminating them until I found the one. Bingo. There it was, he had over a thousand followers and fifty posts; I had like two-hundred followers. I went through his page from vacations in Dubai, Miami and America to business meetings and the gym, his whole life was displayed on his page, I took my time going through the pictures and reading the comments.

I noticed he didn't post anyone apart from himself. There was a particular picture that caught my attention; he was in army green shorts with a white beach shirt. I smiled to myself and double-tapped.

I double-tapped!

I threw my phone and picked it up again. I liked a picture from 2019 in 2022? I was so embarrassed that I quickly logged out of my Instagram and took it as a sign to go to bed already. I could not stop thinking of how terribly I had disgraced myself and why was I thinking about him so much?

My dress was rather tight today, but it was the only thing that did not need ironing plus, it was a Friday, so I did not put in much thought when I wore it. I got to work and settled in, then took the proceedings to the principal. I adjusted my dress to the longest it could be, which was below my knees, before stepping into his office. I was secretly hoping to see you-know-who sitting just like he was the other day, but it was only Mr Okafor with his protruding belly, cucumber in one hand, groundnut on the other, sweating profusely amidst the air conditioner blowing in his office. He eyed me when I walked in and continued to rock his chair.

"Ani-baby," Mr Okafor gushed.

I had told him many times that I thought that nickname was rather inappropriate, but he continuously ignored me.

"Sir, you asked for me?"

"Hmm." His eyes moved from my face and landed on my cleavage. "You are adding o."

I ignored the comment and shifted uncomfortably on my feet.

"Come over here and take the invitation for the award event for Mr Michael Orji's company. We have to represent, and he specially asked for you," Mr Okafor sighed at the last part.

I cautiously moved toward him, and he turned his chair. I moved across the table and kept a safe distance before stretching my hand for the envelope. He moved his hand closer to himself so that when I held the envelope, he dragged me to his lap and held me close. I indeed felt what I was not supposed to feel; I tried to wriggle my way, but that just seemed to be pleasing him.

"You think I don't see what you do, putting on such a dress to tempt me."

He smelt like the mixture of sweat in a busy market afternoon.

"I am a man o! And I am not blind."

I stomped on his leg with my heels, and he let me go. Considering how hard it is to get a job in Nigeria, I had to hold my tongue, I had complained bitterly about Mr Okafor and what he did to junior associates, but the female senior associates said it was the only chance to have a sit on the table, if this was the only chance then I did not want to sit at the table.

"Sir, this is completely inappropriate. The next time

it happens, I will not take it likely." I left his office knowing the punishment that awaited me was going to be lots of unnecessary paperwork and errands. I tried to push what had happened out of my mind and calm my anger, so I opened the invitation card.

I really hope you'll be able to come
P.S wear something red
M

I was grinning from ear to ear. I read the short message over and over, registering his handwriting in my head. It was neat and slanty with a particular curve to it. I quickly put away the letter when I saw Jewel working toward me, he was the office's gossip, and I surely did not want to hear about his plans for the weekend or the people he caught kissing in the coffee room.

"Ah Anne, this dress is the bomb. Is it for your new client?" Jewel asked coyly.

I feigned ignorance and looked everywhere else but his face.

"Ah, the walls have ears, you know. I saw when Michael Orji walked into this office asking everyone for Anne, and I heard that he specifically asked you to handle his company's affairs," Jewel finished with a satisfied grin on his face, hand on his waist.

"I see," was all I said before I excused myself, smiling all the way to the bathroom. *He asked everyone about me*, I thought, smiling to myself.

It was eight-thirty, and I still had not found a decent dress to wear for the award ceremony; my hair was in a high ponytail, and I kept my makeup minimal and classy. As a lawyer, I hardly had any bright clothes - my clothes are mostly black, white, navy blue or ash, so wearing something 'red' was definitely a challenge. It was already too late to buy one, and I was running out of options. I remembered I have sisters and quickly called Sarah; she had worn a tightly fitted red dress with a square neck and a high slit for her engagement party. I rushed to her house and picked it up. Her husband was away; he was a pilot and was barely at home. I slipped on the dress, carried my clutch, and bathed myself in her *Elizabeth Arden* perfume. She made me promise to give her the full gist before I ran out the door.

I was already late, such a terrible impression. The place was hard to find, we had taken a wrong turn, and the driver kept asking me for the location even after I told him to use his map. I stepped out of the car and into the building. I handed my invitation card to the bouncer, and an usher asked me to follow.

The place was dimly lit, apart from the stage, which was the obvious centre of attraction that held all the light, we walked past tables, and she kept going until we were up the stairs and in a private bar with VVIP written on the table. I was going to tap her and tell her she was misunderstood, but when we got there, she showed another bouncer my invitation, and he confirmed it on the list and let me in. The booth was a twelve-seater. Six men were already seated with two other ladies. I greeted and took my seat uncomfortably; no sign of Michael; the ceremony was going on, and people were talking and mingling. I opened my bag and took out my phone and went to my books app, and started reading my eBook. My number one rule was never going to a social event without a book. I was emersed in my book, and I kept flipping pages after pages that I didn't realize someone was watching me.

"Sorry to interrupt, I'm Kehinde Coker," he stretched his hand.

I put my phone away and sat up.

"Nice to meet you, Anne Uchenna."

"Oh, I see you've met Kehinde," a familiar voice rumbled.

I knew that scent. I turned around; he was wearing a black suit with a bright red tie. Red was not the dress code as everyone else was dressed in other colours. I got up and shook his hand.

"I'm happy you could make it." He gave a small smile and still held my hands. Kehinde coughed. Michael sat beside me and turned to the rest of the group: "Guys, meet Anne."

He introduced them to me. They were all friends from university, and they all had their businesses, and we're here to support him; some even flew in from America, as in Kehinde's case, to support him.

"Oh! You're *the* Anne," one of them, Derek added after I was introduced.

I did not know what *Anne* he meant, so I just gave

a puzzled look.

"Oh, Michael has not been able to shut up about the girl he met at the bookstore," Derek explained.

I was blushing so hard; my heart was performing a whole gymnastic routine, but I managed to conceal and give a small smile.

"Okay, that is enough." Michael scratched the back of his head, smiled at me, and then got up to get me something to drink while I continued the conversation with his friends.

The night was slow but fun. I was on my third cup of chapman, I told them I did not drink alcohol, and no one seemed to have a problem with it. Michael was busy, so Kehinde just kept me company. I was finally exhausted; Michael's company had won five awards, and everyone seemed to love him as their cheer got louder each time he came for his award. I excused myself and said goodbye to everyone. They wouldn't let me go, but I explained that I was having a headache and really needed to leave. Kehinde offered to drop me off, but I declined, saying I didn't want him to miss the party because of me.

I looked around for Michael, but I couldn't find him. So, I gave up and stood outside the hotel while I waited for my ride. It was freezing, and I had to hug my arms while standing outside. I felt a heavy material on my shoulders, and I turned to see Michael smiling at me.

"I'm sorry it is a madhouse in there. I didn't realize you left already."

"Oh no, it's completely fine. I had lots of fun. Thank you for inviting me again."

He was looking at me with a sad smile. He fastened the suit on me properly. "I was hoping I would get to spend some time with you tonight. You look absolutely stunning."

"Thank you. I like your tie." I smiled at him.

"I guess you figured out red was not the dress code, and I wanted you to match with me. I'm not sorry for it though."

I smiled, my heart was on a rage, and my knees already weak.

"Truth is, ever since I saw you at that bookstore, I haven't been able to stop thinking about you Anne. I was going to take things slowly, but I don't want to waste your time."

My knees were going to give way. I hoped to fall into his arms, I looked everywhere but his face and when I did, I was lost in those eyes.

"You don't have to say anything. I just wanted to express how I felt... I -"

"I feel the same way," I blurted. Oh, where had my dignity gone. I was supposed to say I'll think about it, so I don't seem easy to have, I looked away, and he smiled.

"It is really cold. Let me drop you at home."

I nodded.

August 5, 2022. I dragged myself out of bed, got ready for work and got out of my room.

"He has not proposed?" my mother asked as she scanned my fingers. I folded them and moved to the table.

"You owe me ten thousand," my mother turned to my sister, who was visiting and scoffed. "I told you, he wouldn't do it before she turned thirty."

My sister frowned and rolled her eyes. My love life had become a bet; I shook my head and started eating; *happy birthday to me.*

The office was even busier, from client to client and with multiple briefs. I was drowning in the work I had to do when my phone beeped.

Happy birthday babe, Dinner at my place?

I smiled at the text. Michael and I had been dating for seven months now. For my birthday, he sent me flowers for a week leading to my birthday; my mom complained that they were no other spaces to keep them, and she wanted a ring, not *vegetables.* I ignored her and arranged them neatly in my room.

This will be the day. I could feel it. I went to the principal by past three p.m. to submit my last files before I grabbed my bag and ran to the nail salon. *I refuse to be proposed to with my nails looking undone.* Just in case, I got them done, bought a new dress and went home. By eight-thirty, I was done with my makeup. I slipped on the gold silk dress and stepped out of my room to total darkness. I moved for the light switch.

"SURPRISE!"

I shifted back and held my chest; I was so scared. I

scanned through the room, my sisters and their husbands, her kids, my mother, Michael and Kehinde with other people I was not so sure I knew, but I was entirely happy. Michael moved forward and hugged me.

"Happy birthday, babe. Will you make me the happiest man in the world and marry me?" He got on his knees and brought out the ring. I was going to cry, but this makeup took hours, and I didn't want to ruin it because of the pictures after. I held them back and nodded frantically.

"Yes, of course! I'll marry you, babe."

We kissed, and the room roared with claps, champagne popping and merriment. My life was a movie.

Our wedding was held in December. Michael wanted it to be in South Africa, so that was where the white wedding was held, while the traditional marriage was in my hometown. We had moved into a new house, and I was still sorting out the last of my things at home.

"No matter what, he is your husband. The two have become one, know that you do not have any room in this house," my mother kept ringing it every time I spoke to her about an argument Michael and I had. One time she said I should stop talking to outsiders about my marriage when I was talking to her, my mother. When did the woman that gave birth to me become an outsider? I stopped talking to her about our arguments.

The first time we had an argument was when I had just got back from work. He had not gone to work that day, and I had been in court all day. I rushed upstairs, got changed and microwaved the stew while I boiled rice before serving it to him.

"Is this today's stew?" he asked after making a funny face at the stew. I had made the stew with other soups the day after our wedding since my office was not willing to give me a break; I had to resume immediately after the wedding, and the work was dumped full force on me as a wedding gift.

"I made it yesterday, but I microwaved it," I replied and got up to taste his stew.

"I do not eat microwaved food. All my meals must be made from scratch."

I looked at him in disbelief. When did this start? I microwaved his food for him all the time when we were dating. How did he expect me to make food every day before and after work?

"Oh, that's almost impossible due to my work schedule. I can reheat the stew if you –"

His hand came crashing on my face. Between the pain and the fact that he slapped me, I couldn't say which one hurt more. I shifted back and held the edge of the table. He stomped off to the room and locked the door. The couch was so uncomfortable, and the mosquitoes fed off my skin all night. The next morning, he got dressed and left his breakfast which was freshly made, untouched. I quickly dressed up and used my powder to cover the red mark that was on my face. I sat at my table in deep thought. I had always said that the last thing I would let a man do was hit me, and there I was, completely lost and confused when the delivery man brought a bunch of roses and delivered them to me.

"Sorry, babe," was all it read.

Who did I marry? The next months helped me to answer this question. I got kicked in the stomach and broke a rib for staining our bed when I was on my period, but he sent a huge teddy bear. I was stepped on numerous times when I did not pick up his calls because I was in court, and he got me a new car. He twisted my fingers when I asked him why he did not wear his wedding ring anymore and got me Gucci shoes.

Our one-year anniversary came, and I kept telling myself every day: *I'm going to leave. I will leave.*

I never did. I could not look at myself in the mirror, such a weak and utterly useless person. I found out I was pregnant three weeks ago, and I had kept it to myself. I told my mom about the abuses first.

"Anita, time is not on your side. There is no need to be sentimental. You don't have a room in this house o! Hmm," was all she told me.

I went back home that day. I held my stomach and decided I was going to tell him; this baby was going to change our lives. I hoped.

After cooking Ogbono soup from scratch as he requested and pounding his yam, I served him that evening.

"I'm pregnant." I smiled at him when I sat beside

him after serving him.

"With whose permission?" he asked, sneering at me.

I struggled to understand the question. Did I need someone's permission to be pregnant with his child?"

"Whose permission?" he repeated, slammed the table, sending the plates and my three hours of hard labour crashing down.

"I am not ready for a child. Get rid of it and make me something else to eat." He got up and left the table.

I followed him into the room. "What do you mean get rid of it, Michael? It is our baby, and I am definitely not getting rid of it." *This baby was very important to me. Why would I abort my baby? Enough is enough*!

I stood my ground,

"Fine. I'll do it for you."

And he did. I saw black and blue when the impact of the kicks reached my belly. I held the bed and struggled to stand up when the stool for the vanity table was destroyed on my back, making me fall again.

Black and blue were all I saw. Sweat, tears and blood flowing from my body. I looked up and saw the man I married; the tears refused to flow. When he stopped and took his car keys, I heard his car drive out. I silently prayed. God was a distant figure to me. I never considered Him but this particular time. I prayed to Him for anything and for nothing, then slowly got up and asked our security to take me to the hospital.

"We really do not know how but the baby is safe. Considering the injuries you sustained, it is almost impossible for the baby to still be alive."

I closed my eyes in tears, and I deeply thanked God. I made a vow to Him to serve him the rest of my days. At that moment, I felt a rush in my spirit, and peace suddenly overwhelmed me. A voice said, 'Anastasia'. I wanted to correct it and say I was Anne, but I did not.

After two weeks, I was discharged, and I headed straight for the police station. The case dragged for months and caused an uproar on Twitter, with comments about how I was only in it out of desperation and was after his money, but I held on. He had connections, but I had a higher force.

Michael was found guilty eight months after I had Anastasia.

"What does this name even mean?" my mother asked.

"Rebirth."

Winnie Enunosowo Eka-Williams, a law student and poet, was born and raised in Cross Rivers State, Nigeria. She loves reading, and when she's not, she's writing. She started writing at the age of 12; it has since been an outlet. She now resides in Abuja, Nigeria, where she has devoted her time to writing and studying and, from time to time, does public speaking.

YOU WERE YOUR MOTHER'S MOTHER

OLIVER SOPULU ODO

It was eke market day. The environment was tranquil, and your mother's exclamation couldn't wait for the cock to crow. Your mother gave birth to you in front of your mother's room. That day became the startling day your father had been waiting for. Your coming took away a painful thirteen-year barrenness.

When you were four years, you enrolled at the king's primary school. You learnt to count the numbers and read the letters your teacher wrote on the blackboard. You were the most brainy in your class. Your teacher called you a foreign machine because of your intelligence.

On one Sunday morning, your mother was preparing you for church, and she saw a mark in your left armpit. Your mother was stunned that she had just discerned the mark in your armpit. She needed your father to see it.

"Honey, oh! Papa Ngozi, come and see oh."

Your father came to your mother's room. Your mother asked your father to sit down. Your mother tried to raise your hand, but you refused to lift your hand up. Your mother stared at you with a smile. You smiled at your mother before your hand was raised by your mother.

"Papa Ngozi nekwa ya, look at it."

Your father looked at your armpit. He saw the mark. He touched your armpit, and you smiled.

"This is just a natural mark by God. It's nothing," your father said and left to his room. Your mother couldn't worry herself again.

You were six years old, and you had transformed into another face. It was not the same face you were born with. And it was a different beautiful face when you were three and five years old. When you were born, people said that you looked like your father, but when you were three and five years old, people said you looked like your mother. But at six years old, you were not alike, neither your father nor your mother. People's prediction about your look-alike was unpredictable.

When you were eight years, you woke up at 1:18 a.m. You walked around your father's house, your eyes were closed, but your mind was opened. Your mother woke up around 1:35 a.m. but didn't see you in your small bed. Your mother stood up and went straight to your father's room, your father who was snoring hard. When your mother didn't see you there, she hit your father.

"Papa Ngozi, I can't find Ngozi."

When your father heard your mother's voice, your father's eyes opened. Your mother and your father rushed outside, and the moon was there; they could see you. You were walking around the house with your eyes closed. They pondered about that, but your mother couldn't waste time but stopped you from going around the house. After that night, you always woke up by 1 a.m.; you woke up for a monologue that was deep to understand.

It was around 1:40 a.m. you woke up, and started a monologue. Your mother was awake. You were sitting down on your bed.

"Nnem! Nnem! The ancestor's body shall disappear someday, but the sun shall rise in the ancestor's head, and the ancestor shall come back to his body, Nnem! Nnem! You shall see blessing again."

Your mother was afraid to hear you. She pondered how a little girl of ten years old could talk to herself. Your mother touched you, and she stared at you.

"Ngozi, what's wrong? Why are you talking to yourself, calling ancestor?"

Your eyes were full of tears, and that made your mother shriek. Your father heard your mother shriek. Your father came to your mother's room.

"What is the problem, Mama Ngozi? Why are you crying?"

Your mother stared at your father then used her wrapper to wipe away her and your tears.

"It is Ngozi," your mother explained.

"Ngozi? What happened to her?"

"Just look at her face. She has been talking since 1 a.m.," your mother replied.

Your father carried you to his room. He kept you at the edge of his bed, your mother came to your father's room, and your mother started praying.

In the morning, your mother went to the house of her friend Mama Emeka. Mama Emeka welcomed your mother and brought a malt drink for her.

"Eunice, Mama Ngozi, you are looking dazed today. What's wrong?" Mama Emeka touched your mother's shoulder. Your mother gave her a bogus smile; she became more worried.

"What's wrong with you? Tell me," Mama Emeka insisted.

Your mother raised her face to stare at mama Emeka. "It's my daughter Ngozi. She has been acting strange for days. I don't really know."

Mama Emeka stared at your mother with a jumbled look then asked, "What's wrong with her?"

Your mother waited a few seconds before she spoke. "She always wakes up around 1 a.m. to talk to herself. And the last thing I heard her say was about ancestor. The other day, I saw her go around the house with her eyes closed."

Mama Emeka looked gloom. "Chineke! Eh! You mean Ngozi has been that eccentric all this time?" mama Ngozi told your mother that Ngozi needed prayers, and she must have rushed you to the pastor for prayers before it was too late.

It was eke market day, again. You became fifteen years old. You slept, and you couldn't wake up. The mark in your armpit disappeared, but no one observed. Your mother cried, but crying couldn't bring you back to life. Your classmates came to your burial. They sang for you, they were holding your picture, singing and crying, but you were not there to hear their cry. They called you Ngozi many times, but you were not there to answer. Your body remained, but your spirit left.

It was Orie market day.

You were given birth to in your grandma's sitting room. After seven days, you were named Chinenyenwa, which means God gives a child. Your mother's pain about Ngozi, who died four years ago, was dismissed by another rebirth of you. Your mother always looked at you and smiled; you were the joy who accepted her after Ngozi left her in so much agony. Your father's elder sister suggested your name. Your father's elder sister said that since it seemed that the devil gave the first one, the name Chinenyenwa could bring a good thing to the child. Your mother wanted you to be named Chinazaekpere. Your father supported his sister.

When you were three years old, you were enrolled at Melody primary school. You started early because your parents wanted you to be stronger.

On your first day, you already knew what some pupils never knew. When your teacher asked the class who could read ABCD, you stood up to read it from A to Z. Everyone was amazed. Your teacher bought cabin biscuits for you, and you shared them with your friends.

When your mother brought you to school the following day, your teacher came closer to greet your mother.

"Good morning, Aunt Eunice, Mama Chinenyenwa, ibula chi?"

Your mother looked up; she saw your teacher smiling at her. She greeted back and smiled. Your teacher came closer to your mother.

"Your daughter is very intelligent. She is so amazing." Your mother smiled. Your mother appreciated that; your mother told your teacher that she started teaching you when you were a year and seven months old. Your teacher appreciated that; your teacher told your mother that you could start primary one by next term.

You became nine years old. You looked more like your father, but when you smiled, you looked like your mother. Your father always made you smile because your father married your mother because of her smile. And your father loved you more when you gave that smile that your mother couldn't give at the time. Your father called you the nickname Chinwa, the short form of your name, and your father touched you on your stomach whenever he wanted to make you smile.

One day your father called you Chinwa. You didn't answer. He touched you. You couldn't smile. You stared at your father with wretchedness, and that made your father scared. Your father asked you the reason why you had refused to smile. You didn't respond. You left your father in his room decorated with your pictures.

2.07 a.m., you woke up. You started crying. Your parents woke up to meet you crying in the sitting room; you had left your mother's room that you had always slept in your mother's bed since you were born.

Emotional, your father touched your face.

"Chinwa, kedu ihe bu nsogbu ghi?"

You stared at your parents. You closed your eyes; you opened your eyes again.

"I am not afraid; I am just scared you are afraid. I am not scared because I am Chinenyenwa. I am God's owner."

You left your mother's room crying.

Your parents went after you.

It was orie market day. You had stomach pain. You screamed. You collapsed on the sitting room tiles, and you never woke up. Your mother fainted, but people were there for her to be saved. It was Ngozi, and it was now Chinenyenwa your mother wept.

Before you were buried, your father brought a kola nut to pray for you. When the youths put you in your grave, your father prayed with the kola nut.

"The God that made us. You have seen us cry again. My grandfather said that the cry of a child is heard by his God. I know you will hear my cry. Ozoemena, let it not happen again. I don't want to see Ngozi and Chinenyenwa again." Your father ended his prayer with a cry. Your father's friend asked him to stop because he was not a woman. Your father's close friend Emeneke told him to cry, but he must not cry like a woman. Emeneke told your father that God had heard his prayers.

It was Afor market day. Afor day was the day of the Umuaji market day. Your mother was screaming for help; your father woke up to help your mother. Your father wanted to take your mother to the hospital, but your mother couldn't move again. Your father went to the house of Mrs Ejikeme, who lived very close to your parent's house. Mrs

Ejikeme came to your mother's room; Mrs Ejikeme found out that your mother was in a critical condition. Mrs Ejikeme called a nurse on the phone - the nurse who also lived nearby.

Some of the women living close to your parents also came by to help your father and Mrs Ejikeme. Before the nurse came, you were born. The women in your mother's room shouted halleluiah and Amen. Your father, who was tired and scared, ran into the room. Your father saw your bloody little self. You were few in complexion. Your father was speechless, and your father embraced every woman in your mother's room.

A minute later, there was a knock. It was from the nurse, who Mrs Ejikeme called on the phone to come. The nurse did every necessary thing that was always given to a woman who just gave birth, and also every necessary thing for a newborn baby.

In eight days, your father invited his kinsmen for your naming ceremony. Your mother suggested the name Kosisochukwu while your father suggested Ogechukwu. Your parents agreed to name you Kosisochukwu, which means the will of God in Igbo language. Your mother suggested the name because three times, she had had children who left her when they grew up.

When you were seven years old, you looked like

your mother. The charming Black skin of your mother, and the voice of your mother, although you were still growing, you had the voice of your mother. Your mother always prayed every midnight for God's protection. Your eyes always became white in the daytime, but at night they became red. Your mother found out about it; she took you to her pastor. Your mother's pastor prayed for you. Your pastor touched your eyes.

"Kosisochukwu, don't be like other of your sisters who left us. Be like another person, not them."

You stared at your pastor with your white eyes. Your pastor smiled at you, but you couldn't smile. You were not happy; you were hungry and tired. Your mother told you to say thank you to your pastor, which you refused to say.

When you were ten years old, your parents organized a birthday party. Some of your friends came, and also some of your classmates. That day made you happy since you were born. Your parents found out about your happiness, they thought your happiness could make you stay alive, but a dead tree didn't need water to live. And you were the dead tree in the body of a human. You were growing up with a smile inside but with blues in your armpit.

You were fourteen years old. You became a good Artist. You drew your mother and your father, even your teacher. Your mother and your father appreciated your drawing. Your teacher also appreciated it. One day you drew a woman that looked like your grandmother. When your mother was washing your school bag, your mother saw the drawing in your drawing book. She screamed.

"Kosisochukwu, who is this woman?"

You came to meet your mother in the corridor. You stared at your drawing, but you started crying. Your mother didn't know why you were crying. She asked you. You stared at her.

"Mummy, I drew myself. It's myself."

Your mother was amazed to hear that. She smiled at you.

"Kosi, have you seen yourself in a mirror before?"

You wanted to leave your mother when she asked you that question, but she stopped you by holding your hand. She embraced you. She looked into your eyes.

"Kosi, you drew someone who looks like my mother. But it's not you. It's my mother. Both of you don't look alike. My mother was my best friend."

It was Afor day. Your mother had prepared your birthday gift on the ninth day of the month of March, a day before your birthday. Your mother prayed from 12:12 a.m. to 5.09 a.m.. She called you Kosi. You woke up at 6.13 a.m. to prepare for school. Before you left for school, your mother prayed for you. She promised you that when you got back, she would give you a birthday gift she bought for you. You left with the happiness of the birthday gift that your mother promised to give you. But you couldn't return from school. You were hit by a car when crossing the last road to your home. Your body was on that ground with blood around you. But your soul was no more with you. You had broken your parents' hearts again. But it was the will of God according to your mother.

It was six months since you left your parents a third time. Your parents found out that there was a reason dogs always barked at midday. Your mother went to the pastor to pray for her one Wednesday afternoon. Your mother's pastor already knew the reason for the visit. Your mother stared at the pastor with a bored face. The pastor told your mother to sit down. Your mother started crying, her head lying on the pastor's table.

"Sister Eunice, you don't have to cry. God is already in control. Rise up and listen to me."

Your pastor touched your mother on her shoulder. Your mother was still weeping. Your mother raised up her head, this time to look at the pastor. She used her wrapper to clean her tears.

"Pastor, pastor, you know, three times I have had children, who died anytime they were fifteen years, it's not bad to cry so God can see my tears. I could die if I don't cry, pastor."

The pastor stood up from his seat again to come closer to your mother.

"It is bad. It's ok. God has already seen your tears. Remember what the Bible says in Psalm 121, God is your helper. You don't need to cry no more." Your pastor told your mother to pray that the devil's plans should fail.

Your father had been in a chaotic situation ever since

your mother was six months pregnant. Your father was visited by an old friend who was living in Abuja. Your father's friend, Mr Benjamin, had already heard everything about your father's situation. Mr Benjamin advised your father to meet a seer to know the root of the problem. Your father accepted Mr Benjamin's advice. Your father pleaded with Mr Benjamin to take him to the seer at Abeano. Mr Benjamin agreed to take him to the seer's place.

It was on Saturday morning. Your father and Benjamin came to seer's place. Your father and Benjamin waited for three hours before it was time for them to see the seer. Your father and Mr Benjamin were ordered by a boy to come inside the seer's room. Your father and Benjamin came inside the seer's room, they saw the seer turning his back to them, but the seer told them to sit down.

"You're welcome, my brothers. I can see that you need spiritual eyes to see what's beyond the world. But I must tell you. You are in the right place. But does a man see more than the world? The answer is no. No. A man is a man. A man needs extra eyes to see above the world. I just need the person that has a problem to say I am the one," the seer spoke with a deep voice that sounded twice in the ears of your father and his friend Mr Benjamin. They were scared. Your father waited for a few seconds before he spoke.

"I am the one," your father answered, looking at the back of the seer. Your father expected the seer to turn to face him, but the seer didn't turn his face to them.

"Listen, you have a problem. Your child keeps coming back to you. Although she came back with a different face, she was still the one. She will continue to come back until she is taken out in the afterlife. I can tell you that your child is your mother-in-law. She loved your mother. She was killed because she was a fearless woman. She still wants to live, but the dead can only live only where there is rebirth. Go and wait for her rebirth and death. It may come so soon." The seer got up and went away.

Your father and MrBenjamin were scared. They went out, looked around and found out no one was there, and everywhere was silent.

Your father didn't tell your mother about what the seer told them because your father knew that your mother could take away her life if she found out. Your father had stopped sleeping in the middle of the night. He always woke up to think. Benjamin had already advised him to leave his village in Enugu state to go to Abuja with his wife because the village could be a bad place to stay.

Your mother accepted your father's plead to go to Abuja with him. At this time, she was seven months pregnant.

It was Nkwo market day. Your father took your mother to Holy Mother Hospital at 4.13 a.m. Your mother delivered a baby girl. You were the baby girl. You had come the fourth time. This time around. You were more beautiful, and you had those charming eyes. You started smiling since you were born. Your mother was happy, but she was afraid if you were still the same child. Your mother's happiness couldn't reach her full heart. Your father was trying to be happy; even when the doctor told him that his wife had given birth, your father didn't rejoice. The doctor was amazed because he expected your father to be happy.

In eight days, you were named Chinwe, which means God's own. Your mother always remembered the Dreams she always had when she was pregnant. Your mother always saw her dead mother smiling at her in the dream. Sometimes, your mother's mother could come in the dream, kissing your mother's pregnant belly. But your mother couldn't notice any strange thing about that. The memory of that always made your mother smile every time she looked at you, your face that is now becoming your grandmother's face.

When your mother was preparing you for school one Monday morning, she found a mark in your armpit. It was the second time she'd seen that mark. Your mother didn't know that you had had the mark anytime she had a child. Your mother remembered that she had seen the mark in her first child. She was scared again. She called your father to come and see the mark, but your father refused to come. Your father pretended to be sleepy that day.

On one Sunday morning, you were seven years at the time. Your mother called you to come, and she found out that you looked like her mother. The face of her mother, the voice of her mother, the smile, and the black beauty of her mother. Your father came inside the sitting room with four beers. Your father smiled at you. It was a phoney smile. Your father wanted to smile because he wanted to show your mother that he didn't hate you as your mother thought.

"Papa Chinwe, your daughter looks like my mother. Have you found out?"

Your father nodded. Your father knew it was not a good thing because the seer had already said that his children had been his mother-in-law. Your father left the sitting room to his room.

Abuja city had been a good place for your father, who had started a big provision business. Your father had been doing well, and your father had also enrolled you in the best secondary school. This time your father had been waiting for your time. Your father didn't tell his relatives about the reason for his children's death anytime his children were fifteen years old. Although his relatives had been telling him to marry a new wife; some of them called your mother a witch. It had been the best place for your parents to live.

You were fifteen years old. Your parents had counted it. The day of your birthday, your parents waited for you to leave like the others. You couldn't go to school. You were sick. You were sleeping all that day. The next day, you came to your mother. Your mother stared at you.

"Are you Ngozi?" your mother asked.

You stared at your mother.

"Who is Ngozi?' you asked.

Your mother was still staring at you.

"Are you Chinenyenwa?" your mother came closer to you.

You were staring at her. You couldn't move.

"Mum, who is Chinenyenwa?" you were wondering.

"Or, are you Kosisochukwu?" your mother asked.

You started crying this time. You wanted to go, but your mother embraced you.

It was twenty years. And you were still alive. Your parents had been wondering. You were in your third year at the University of Nigeria, Nsukka. You were studying English and Literary Studies. Your parents were pleased. Whenever your mother looked at your face, you reminded her about her mother. You were beautiful. You were the boy's favourite because of your beauty. Suitors had started coming, but you refused because you wanted to finish your university before you get married. You were not only beautiful but intelligent. When you won a beauty contest at the University of Nigeria, Nsukka, your parents were glad.

You were asked by a student at the time if you were the daughter of a mermaid? You left the place. The boy is a seer, but he had never discovered it. The boy saw your eyes change colours; it changed from red to green in seconds. But you left when the boy asked the question.

It was in your final year, the last day of your exam, and you were wearing a white polo. Your eyes were white at the time. You have already told your parents that the day was your last exam. Your parents asked you to come back three days after your last exam, so they could celebrate with you. Your father sent you a lovely message:

"I am happy for this time you are no other ones.
You are another.
Congratulations in advance, dearest daughter."

You read the message. You smiled. Your mother called you, and you spoke with your mother. You were happy that day. You went for your last exam by 3 p.m. The exam was to start at 4 p.m., but the exam started by 4.18 p.m. You finished your exam by 5:35 pm. You stood up to submit your exam script and fell.

That was the end of you.

Oliver Sopulu Odu is a Nigerian writer who has published works in Okadabooks. He participated in the Chinua Achebe memorial Anthology and End SARS Anthology both organized by society of Young Nigerian Writers in 2020; his poem is published in J.J Rawlings memories and Mementos Anthology 2021 and a flash fiction that's longlisted for Engaging Borders Africa.

ABOUT KEP

OTHER KEP TITLES

NOTES
ON LOVE
& OTHER
STORIES
VINE 2022
KEPRESSNG
ANTHOLOGY
PRIZE
KEPRESSNG ANTHOLOGY PRIZE
FLIP-FLOP

CONTACTS

Thank you for purchasing this book.
I hope you enjoyed it.
For more, let's meet at any of these places.

Facebook: https://www.facebook.com/kepressng
Instagram: https://www.instagram.com/kepressng
For newsletters: https://www.kepressng.com

ABOUT US

Kemka Ezinwo Press (KEP) Ltd is an African publishing company with the vision of broadening the power of African literary works and compositions. Our aim is to remind the world that we're avid readers, and to combat the self-imposed superstitions that Africans don't read.

Our core values are Excellence, Collaboration, Discovery, & Generosity.

To launch our officially opening, we decided to introduce the KepressNG Anthology prize, a collection of shorts from debut and veteran authors with African lineage multi-collection. We incorporated our Vision of developing and increasing African literature by making it a competition for the selection of the best story.

The KepressNG Anthology prize is designed for teenagers, though not restricted to them, to write stories that they'd hope to read. Our stories matter and who better than us to tell our stories. Societies change and the most affected are the young.

The idea of tying the story to a theme is our way of helping new and emerging authors establish a discipline of telling us the story without the faff.

The prose is in short form and not restricted to a specific genre.

There's a belief that short stories are a thing of the past but most young adult start out with short stories. Should we now abandon them in the abyss and or anarchy of the literary formation proficiency?

As an anthology prize giver, we want to rebuild the reinstate the idea that writing is lucrative if only to the individual's aesthetics thereby building better mental health and expanding knowledge.

RULE OF ENTRY INTO THE KEPRESSNG ANTHOLOGY PRIZE

Calling all would-be writers, unpublished or self-published African writers, to our second KEPRESSNG ANTHOLOGY 2022 PRIZE titled JUVENILE.

Ten lucky winners will:
~Be published in an anthology.
~Get five complimentary copies of the anthology, amongst other prizes.

TERMS & CONDITIONS

Entry is free, but you must be African or of African descent.
Your entry must be in English; it can be fictional or non-fictional.
Your entry or entries must follow the chosen theme.

All entries must be submitted in MS Word format, double line spaced in TIMES ROMAN font.
~Your name must not appear in the body of the story.
~The entry must be between 3,000 and 10,000 words.
~ Your submission email title must be as follows: JUVENILE - TITLE OF YOUR STORY - AUTHOR NAME.
~All entries must be received by Midday on the 2nd of July 2022 (WAT).
~The winners will be announced on the 23rd of July, 2022.
~Please give details if the story has been published elsewhere.

Send your submissions & FAQs to kemkaezinwo.press@gmail.com.

Good luck.

SNEAK PREVIEW

CAPTURED WITHIN – KEMKA EZINWO

Prologue

Teenage lovers littered the little bank of *Kono* waterside. It was probably the hottest day in the history of that small village in the middle of the southern part of Nigeria. The older people - parents and grandparents - took refuge under all the orange and mango trees, even the guava trees; Very few people had verandas or sheds. The children didn't have a place to hide their heads from the penetrating sun rays; those that did were not permitted to share with their parents lest they got wind of the latest gossip or 'adult entertainment'. Even the place Livinus discovered was taken over by Mfon and Tonye who in turn chased them away, but not before Ambrose tied the mangoes and oranges in his shirt; He did this to prevent Matthew from spoiling his only shirt while Livinus packed his *efuru*: weevil larva.

Ambrose discovered a new place, a mile off, on the opposite side of Livinus' dethroned spot. To ensure that no one seized it, Ambrose made them walk along tall elephant grasses and covered their footprints with leaves and twigs. They arrived what looked look like an abandoned clearing, with moderately tall trees scattered around like a curved mosaic. On the ground were ankle-high rust-coloured leaves. Matthew made a broom with long thin twigs. He had just about finished sweeping when he hit the heel of his left foot on something hard. He made the sign of the cross: hitting your left foot on something was believed to be a bad omen. Livinus, being the least cautious one, pulled Matthew back and tried to dig the round mould out unsuccessfully then Ambrose knocked on it as you would knock on a door. Frustrated, they let it be.

"That's odd," Ambrose muttered.

"What is?" Matthew asked casually.

"The leaves on my side are wet."

"So?" Livinus asked, somewhat irritated. He had spent the whole time walking around them, doing nothing.

"Well," Ambrose emphasized. "It hasn't rained for days and even if it did, all the leaves should be wet too."

Matthew blinked. "Yes. There might be water somewhere."

Livinus stepped out of the way and watched make a track free of leaves.

The water was three feet high in a red brick runway, with one end shaped like a spoon and the middle of it like a decorative bowl made from concrete. Livinus went to the bowl to remove the leaves, but when he saw the way the leaves kept rising and falling like breathing, he backed away quietly. Meanwhile, Ambrose pulled weeds from around the stream and along its walls, and Matthew removed the leaves from the water with the broom.

Matthew went to the decorative bowl to remove the leaves from there too. The water squirted on his face. Unable to stop the water's tirade, he stepped aside to stare at it. It was the first time he had seen anything like that. It was a fountain.

Their desire to discover the source of the water flow was drenched by the cool breeze and their tired limbs. The sunlight did not penetrate the thick canopy of leaves, so they lay down supporting their head with their arms.

"We can do more cleaning tomorrow, what do you think?" Matthew asked.

Ambrose dipped his index finger into the water and tasted it, then bolted upright and cried, "It's clean water o!"

After lapping some water, one after the other they jumped in and started splashing it on each other. Livinus was the first to step out after about an hour. Ambrose's eyes fell on something as he climbed out but didn't want to alert Livinus just in case he would lead them to another default palpitation from the scourge of a cane; it was unlikely for Livinus to stay out of trouble of which he was never a victim.

Livinus crossed his arms and stared in awe and admiration at their discovery. "Do you know how rich the former owner must have been to spend money on this?"

"Why did you say former?" Matthew asked, wrinkling his nose as he brushed water off his face.

"Will you have something like this and abandon it?"

Matthew shrugged.

"It depends," Ambrose murmured.

"I'm going to be a rich man I promise you!" Livinus said sitting on a slab beside the stump of the cashew tree scratching his leg.

"We all want to be rich!" Ambrose responded as he washed the mangoes and set three aside.

"No! You're not listening. I mean I must be rich. To God, I'll do anything!"

"Be careful what you wish for!" Ambrose said as he joined them under the tree.

"What will you do if you are rich?" Ambrose asked Matthew and passed a mango to him.

"I'll take my mother to a new and large house and buy her anything she wants. What about you?"

"I don't know. I haven't thought of it before… maybe I should travel to a place where I would not see Papa, the drunkard."

"Let nobody hear you call him that o!"

Ambrose twisted his mouth then whispered, "What do you think Livinus will do when he gets rich?"

"Buy new clothes?"

"I think he will pay people to look for trouble," Ambrose retorted, nodding.

Matthew shook his head, smiling, still not understanding Livinus' and Ambrose's attitude towards each other.

Livinus paced from one place to another, breaking off branches as he walked along the tall elephant grasses. Ambrose and Matthew delved into their mangoes.

Livinus with eager eyes that looked like they were about to be separated from their sockets said: "Let's agree that whoever gets rich first will sponsor the others to get to where he is."

Ambrose and Mathew looked at each other, shrugged and chorused, "Okay!"

After locking pinkies, they went back to their mangoes, except Livinus who returned to pacing. A few minutes later they looked back, wondering why they hadn't heard Livinus murmuring for a while. When they didn't see him, they shared his mango among themselves and kept the ones they were taking back close to their makeshift stools.

Matthew suddenly looked back at the trees. "Wait o! Do you know the way out of here?"

"Yes, I marked the path we took. Where is that boy now? Let him not get us into another trouble o! Livinus has gone to look for trouble I'm sure!"

Trouble hmn! Matthew thought and remembered what his mother said on his birthday *'Son, they will always come and confront me because we are poor. Please stay away from Livinus for your own sake eh! He is a bad influence.'*

"Matthew, I saw something earlier. Come, I'll show you!"

They went and cleared the slab. It was an old well. The inscription on it read:

This is where we met.

This is where our hearts became one.

They may never let us be together, but we'll always live together here.

This is where we'll be, and this is where we'll rest.

Carlton Benedict Bernwick & Idongesit Ekpeyong

1953

"Who do you think they are?" Ambrose asked.

"That is a stupid question. I don't even think my mother was born back then."

"Did I not say 'former'?" Livinus asked in an attempt to brag.

Ambrose and Matthew laughed, still staring at the inscription. Livinus fumed, saying nothing as he hurried towards the path they had taken to the clearing.

Ambrose noticed. "Be ready, because Livinus will get us into trouble again. I still feel the pain from the last time." Ambrose winced as he rubbed his upper arms.

"Don't think like that *nawh*!" Matthew pleaded.

"Why shouldn't I eh? You see, you believe anything he tells you. Livinus is only interested in Livinus, and the only reason he comes back to us is that you will tag along, and I'll have to follow you and also because -" Ambrose looked ahead and shook his head.

"But -"

"But he can do it and get away with it. After all, his father makes sure that anyone who touches him will leave this village before nightfall. No oh! Instead, he will come and drag us into it."

"Why?" Matthew asked, as he threw pebbles into the water and counted the ripples.

"Because he enjoys watching us suffer."

Ambrose joined him after tying the remaining fruits in his t-shirt. They were still counting ripples when they heard the rustling of leaves. It stopped, and they returned to ripple-counting. They scrambled to their feet when they heard stumping of footsteps and Livinus shouting, "Run!"

"Told you!" Ambrose said.

"Not again!" Matthew cried, sounding scared.

Ambrose was afraid that they might not get out in time, so soon after he tied the t-shirt around his waist, he dragged his friend with one hand, and with his free hand covered the slab they sat on with sand, leaves, and twigs, and whispered, "We have to hide!"

While they lay in the grass hiding, Livinus ran to the spot they had just covered. When he didn't see them, he remained standing to wait for his chasers to catch up with him. His chasers all looked at him and eventually started walking away, except for a very fair woman who was as round as the kettle drum in the church; she slapped him and pulled him by the ear. She wouldn't let go until the others with mixed feelings insisted that she made him go. Soon after she let Livinus go, they left the same way they came.

Livinus called out to his friends, but they didn't come up. A few seconds passed before Livinus hurried after the group of people that has chased him.

"Let's go now before the night catches up with us," Ambrose said.

Ambrose and Matthew laughed all the way home as they recounted the event. Then they branched off to their houses.

*****

In the excitement, Matthew told his mother, Eka-Matty, everything and she laughed, shaking her head simultaneously.

"You're lucky that you had Ambrose with you." Eka-Matty sighed shaking her head. *When will my son learn?* "School tomorrow; bed now."

"But Mummy!"

"Bed now!"

"Yes mummy…" he rose from the cane chair that was once his father's, reluctantly, "…good night!"

"Hmn goodnight!" she replied and watched her son exit the sitting room but got distracted by the knock on her door. There was a tear-stricken dishevelled young lady at the door.

"Udeme? Come in! Come in!" Eka-Matty stepped aside to let Udeme in. "What happened?"

They barely sat down before Udeme burst into tears. Eka-Matty crossed the centre-table, sat beside Udeme and rocked her until she was sober.

"What happened?"

"It's him o! And as always, she has taken his side. She even went as far as saying that I can divorce him if I don't like him... I want to get married and stay married that is why I must marry someone I can manage with you know," Udeme spoke between sniffles. "Why can't she understand that? Eh?"

Eka-Matty sighed.

Udeme got up abruptly startling Eka-Matty. "Aunty good night!"

"You just got here," Eka-Matty said, reluctantly getting up.

"Yes, but I'm going. I just got this marvellous idea. I'll tell you of the outcome when I'm done."

"Just make sure you don't do anything stupid."

"I won't Aunty. I promise I won't."

One

The crispy august wind smacked Matthew Udoh. He could barely see through the fog, let alone find the aluminium bucket. He hated the harmattan season because his skin would shrivel like the smoked mackerel his mother bought for dinner and then itch for hours. Should he open his mouth, his already chapped lips would tear; the last time it took weeks to heal. The sun wasn't out. He trembled at the thought of pouring cold water over his body. He shuddered: the escaping moon cast its reflection on the surface of the water in the bucket, reminding him of its icy coldness. Lifting a bowl full of water, he held his breath and threw the water over himself. The water landed on the ground with a light thud, splinters of it touching his feet – he had shifted before the water fell. His mother's voice echoed, rekindling the courage he needed.

I need oil on my skin, he thought, then winced touching his cheeks as the memory of when Eka-Effiòng's hand harshly stroked his cheek resurfaced – he heard chirping much like the little blue birds that circled 'Tom's head in the *Tom and Jerry* cartoon, which he and his friends had watched through a crack in the door of Ette Okon's house. He never understood how such a frail-looking woman could lash out such pain.

"I'll never take what doesn't belong to me again!" he muttered to himself.

Thinking of *Tom and Jerry*, he smiled. Ette Okon would never have discovered how rats started getting into his house if Livinus had not gone bragging to his sisters.

His skin had started to itch, but he couldn't get his hands through his clothes because they were snug.

"Matty! Ekamba eyen mmi!" his mother shouted from the back of the house. He could tell she was coming out of the bathroom from the sound of the zinc door.

"Have you eaten your food?" she asked in *Ibibio* language.

She always brought a smile to his face, probably because she was the only family he had or because she was easy to talk to. He was once told that his mum was the belle of the village, that she stood tall among her peers – still did, with long, black and glossy hair, that the superstitious suspected she was a *'mammy water'*. She was slender, and her dark skin glowed, her eyes shaped like cat's eyes stamped with hazel-coloured pupils. She had a small, pointed nose, and her lips were small, all neatly tucked in an oval-shaped face. Nobody understood what she saw in his father - one minute he was in a good mood and then another he was in a bad mood - no one knew about bipolar disorder then. Matthew was told he had his mother's looks, though he didn't see how.

His skin started itching again.

He rushed to where his food was, and his eyes lit with joy. It was *garri* and palm kernel. His jaws hurt as he chewed, but he didn't care. It was like eating rice and chicken on Christmas day. He hurriedly ate his food as he didn't want his friends to see him soaking *garri*. Nevertheless, he couldn't help waiting for the *garri* to swell.

Matthew's mother, Matty, she was so called because it was shorter than calling her Eka-Matty, watched her son eat with relish and smiled and murmured, "Thank you, Jesus!" For weeks, they'd been eating cooked unripe pawpaw. She knew he ate it to please her. He didn't beg, which often surprised her. She turned towards the door she was leaning on to hide her tears and pray. *Please, God. Look not on my sins. Look on the faith I have in you and take my son away from this misery. Please don't let him grow up in poverty.*

"Mummy, I have finished eating o," Matthew said and wiped his mouth.

Smiling, she wiped away her tears.

"Mmami, thank you."

"You're welcome, dear child. I have a surprise for you."

Eka-Matty undid one end of her wrapper, loosening the tip to reveal scrunched-up money. She gave it to him. She opened the door to withdraw something in a black cellophane bag: it was a pair of slippers. The money was from the sale of palm kernel: it wasn't enough to cover both his school fees, and a pair of sandals. Matthew jumped up and down in excitement, and then wiggled his waist and jumped on his mother who started laughing. He was glad to be paying his fees on the first day of school; something that had never happened before. Although he couldn't wear the slippers in school, it would protect his feet from the hot roads to and from school.

His friends, Livinus Orhiunu and Ambrose Livingstone, arrived just as he was putting the money into his pocket. Livinus was talkative and chubby in an intimidating way; even the senior prefects feared to flog him whenever he was late. His father even suspected him of stealing food at night. His father never caught him because he did it in the afternoon.

Ambrose, on the other hand, was lanky, reserved and taller than most people his age with four older brothers, of which three were now late, and seven sisters. His mother and Matthew's mother got along but weren't friends, which was expected as Ambrose's mother was old enough to be Matthew's mother.

They arrived at school late because Livinus had forgotten something, again. Mr Kalabór, the duty Master for the day, and the Labour all year round was at the school entrance with his *koboko.* The staff and pupils of Saint Barnabas Primary School, Kono didn't take kindly to this his *koboko.* No one openly objected because Mr Kalabór was related to the Headmaster. However, some teachers shielded their children and played the 'mind-your-business' game when it came to the other pupils.

Mr Kalabór, a lanky man, with a large, hooked nose that seemed to overwhelm his face, glared sternly at them. "Why are you always late? I let you pass yesterday, but that is not happening today. Kneel!"

Matthew was already shaking like a leaf under heavy rain. He gave everyone six strokes of his *koboko,* but when it got to Matthew's turn, he frowned, maybe because he was afraid the boy would die. He quickly thought of a way to protect his reputation.

Mr Kalabór hissed at Matthew. "Come with me!"

Matthew followed.

When they got to the staffroom, his frown was replaced with concern.

"Sit down. Are you all right?" Mr Kalabór asked softly.

Matthew's reply was inaudible. His eyes glazed, his mouth watered as the different aromas of displayed food hit him. A staff on maternity leave had sent food from the celebration of the safe delivery of her first son. Mr Kalabór noticed how the little boy's eyes danced from one dish to another, offered to get him some food but Matthew refused. Mr Kalabór got a paper plate and filled it up.

"I won't tell if you won't," Mr Kalabór whispered.

Before Mr Kalabór could say, 'A', Matthew was slurping and gulping away with such speed that the star-nosed mole would envy, and a grass cutter would relish. He had just finished eating and was wiping his mouth with the back of his hand when a light-skinned girl walked in, pulled by the ear into the room by Miss Boyd.

The girl looked a lot like her even though Miss Boyd's face was covered in pimples.

He remembered he had seen her with Mfon when he went with his mother to sell palm kernel. He remembered her because she kept wrinkling her face as if she was trying to get her mouth to cover her nose. She was so thin it looked like a feather could knock her down, with her nose as pointy as the cones they were told to make in class the last term, and her hair was brown and curly. Her skin shone like Ette Okon's Sunday shoes after it had been waxed with the Kiwi shoe polish, which he claimed was a souvenir.

She must be the new girl that Livinus' sisters were talking about yesterday; I can almost swear they were jealous.

He stared at her, and only realised his mouth had been open when he accidentally swallowed something: *saliva, a fly?*

She giggled, covering her mouth to muffle the sound.

He looked over at Miss Boyd, whose hand was still on the girl's ear. Frowning, he tried to remember her name.

The Labour Master came in, saw Matthew and grunted, "Don't you have a class you should be in?"

Before the teacher could utter another word, Matthew ran as fast as his wobbling legs could carry him. He couldn't understand why his legs were suddenly wobbly.

*****

From where she stood, Annette could see the boy who was as thin as she was run to his class. It was her class too. *Very white teeth for a village boy!* She thoughts and twisted her mouth dispassionately as she tried to clean her teeth with her tongue. She had been staring at him and only realised that Miss Boyd was in class when she saw the heads of her classmates through the window – an indication that they were all standing. She ran as fast as she could and got into the class just as Miss Boyd called out her name.

"Annette Orlu."

"Present!" Annette answered, standing by her seat.

Miss Boyd looked up, noticing that Annette was standing, although she knew that Annette wasn't late for school. Not caring for whatever reason her niece might have had for being betwixt, she gave her two strokes of the cane. Annette wanted to explain to the teacher that someone was on her seat; through the tears, she pleaded with Livinus to give up her seat, and he merely looked at her like she was stupid. Matthew beckoned her over. She picked up her bag which had been dislodged, dusted it and went over two desks to sit with Matthew. Livinus was furious but said nothing.

Miebi Livingstone, Ambrose's twin sister had always considered herself an advocate ever since she talked Livinus' father into not smacking his son for taking his travelling bag to school. Who knew the father had changed his mind because he intended to use the money for his son's Christmas gift to replace the tattered thing? She had equally appointed herself advocate for her classmates – as an aspiring politician. She made it a point to introduce herself to everyone, especially new pupils. She didn't care how loud the din, the louder she was, the better. It came as no surprise when she approached Matthew's desk during the break period with her somewhat reluctant best friend, Mfon.

Miebi struck her chest. "My name is Miebi! I know your name is Annette! This is my friend, Mfon!"

"We have already met." Mfon retorted sharply.

"Oh, okay. Well, I'm going to ease myself." Miebi stamped her feet angrily and briskly walked away.

Mfon watched Miebi leave and almost hissed. No one really understood Mfon, she was friends with Miebi, and then they weren't friends. It had gone on for as long as they existed, so much so that everyone became an observant bystander. She rarely spoke to anyone, but Miss Boyd had brought Annette over their house at the weekend two weeks before school opening. She rolled her eyes as she watched Miebi leave the class and turned to face Annette. They talked for some time before walking out of the classroom. Mfon made a personal declaration to make school a little bit bearable for Annette when she found out that she hated school.

Annette, on the other hand, was a bit distracted. Her focus was on Matthew, who was playing football with his friends. She found him weird. He dragged his feet when he walked, though he stood tall. He drooled when he spoke, and his head looked droopy like her Uncle's own did anytime he fought with his female friends. She loved the way he talked like he was counting his words; unlike her father, whose speech was like gurgling water.

Livinus wanted to get back at Matthew for stealing his chance of talking to Annette, that he kicked the ball hard towards Matthew who deftly dodged it. It went flying in the direction of the girls who sat at the edge of the field and landed in

Annette's food and in turn desecrated her white school uniform.

Horrified, Livinus ran towards them, then came to a halt a few meters from them in case one of them would lash out like his sisters usually did.

Mfon reprimanded Livinus and hushed Annette when she started to whimper.

"I am really sorry. I didn't mean to," Livinus pleaded.

They didn't believe Livinus, not after his action in the classroom. He looked gloomy with his slumped shoulders as they sneered or hissed when he passed by. He felt so bad that he prayed that the day would pass quickly. That day, he was the first out of the class when school was over, but the last in the line for devotion. As they sang, '*Now the day is over…*' he looked at Matthew scornfully.

Printed in Great Britain
by Amazon